NOT ENOUGH INDIANS

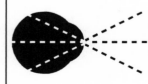 This Large Print Book carries the
Seal of Approval of N.A.V.H.

NOT ENOUGH INDIANS

HARRY SHEARER

THORNDIKE PRESS

An imprint of Thomson Gale, a part of The Thomson Corporation

THOMSON

™

GALE

Detroit • New York • San Francisco • New Haven, Conn. • Waterville, Maine • London

THOMSON
GALE™

LIBRARY OF CONGRESS CATALOGING-IN-PUBLICATION DATA

Shearer, Harry, 1943–
    Not enough Indians / by Harry Shearer.
        p. cm. — (Thorndike Press large print laugh lines)
    ISBN-13: 978-0-7862-9264-6 (lg. print : alk. paper)
    ISBN-10: 0-7862-9264-4 (lg print : alk. paper)
    1. Indians of North America — Fiction. 2. Casinos — Fiction. 3. Large type
books. 4. New York (State) — Fiction. I. Title.
    PS3619.H4325N68 2007
    813'.54—dc22   2006035003

Published in 2007 by arrangement with Writer's House Publishers, Inc.

Printed in the United States of America on permanent paper
10 9 8 7 6 5 4 3 2 1

This book is dedicated to Dora, who inspires me with her strength and her writing, and to Judith, who inspires me with everything she does, except watching *Law and Order.*

ACKNOWLEDGMENTS

Much of this book was written in New Orleans. Portions were written in Fiji, and my thanks to Gavin de Becker for being such an unobtrusive host (were you actually there?). Thanks also to Tom Leopold, Melanie Greene, Karen Stabiner, Mark Childress, Victor Rocha, John and Lynn Fischbach (we'll always have Biloxi), Pam Halstead, and Delaune Michel.

THE CHARACTERS

GAMMAGE/FILAQUONSETT RESERVATION, NEW YORK

Curtis Zorn: the Mayor/Chief, mid-thirties, a slightly built, sandy-haired technocrat's technocrat lost in a world where all the logical easy fixes have failed.

Barbara Menzies: a fortyish Selectperson (like your City Council member) gifted with a blunt directness, a plus-sized man trapped in a plus-sized woman's body.

Casey Elliott: another Selectperson, a sweet-tempered man in his late thirties who affects the pony-tailed appearance of the aging hippie he's too young to be.

Earlene Hammond: the British-accented, New York-born general manager of the local public radio station, who does pledge drive pitches in her sleep.

Daria Halperin: pear-shaped in the best of times, a one-time student activist turned local busybody. In her mid-forties, she

9

wears her hair in the style of a slightly used Brillo pad.

Dick Dirigian/Stillwater: a balding, slightly paunchy, single man in his early fifties, Dick is affably glib enough to sell gas ovens to Auschwitz survivors.

Dr. Roger Gardner: stern of visage and voice, always dressed in three-piece black suits, Dr. Gardner is head of the Gammage School District and, thanks to his own tireless efforts, known as the smartest man in town.

Las Vegas, Nevada

Anthony (Tony) "Loose Slots" Silotta: the black-haired, handsome, smooth-talking self-described King of Vegas Class, he has built, owned, and lost control of half the hotels on the Strip, and he's not through yet.

Serena (Reeny) Silotta: Tony's hand-selected trophy wife, plucked from the world of Vegas dancers to live a life of caged luxury.

Wowosa Reservation, Connecticut

Joseph Catspaw (Né Katz): a spiky-haired Jewish Indian in his late forties, who started in the fashion jeans business and now finds himself running the world's largest Native American casino.

Don Nightswim: a mysterious African American with just a hint of Native American blood who, when he's not living at least one alternate life, is Joseph's right-hand Indian.

WASHINGTON, D.C.

Vince Winstanley: a crew-cut straight arrow in his fifties, a longtime denizen of the Interior Department bureaucracy. His wife, a prim charmer in her late forties named Eileen, is an art consultant for schools and corporations. They raise and show Dobermans.

Hap Matthews: Vince's boss at the Bureau of Indian Affairs, a man in his early sixties who would fade into the woodwork if only the woodwork weren't so colorful.

■ ■ ■ ■

PART ONE

■ ■ ■ ■

1

THE TOWN OF GAMMAGE, NEW YORK SEPTEMBER 1996

The meeting had lasted for hours. Adrenalized by the crisis atmosphere in the room and, indeed, in the town, citizen after citizen had marched to the podium and tinkered with the goosenecked microphone, sending a painful array of mechanical groaning noises through the public-address system. Finally satisfied with mike-to-mouth relationship, as one, they denounced in thrilling varieties of fiery language the proposed city garbage tax.

"Just exactly what are we supposed to do?" the ideologically plain Lucy Striker demanded, her voice rising to a quasi-operatic shriek, "Eat our trash?"

"You people," the elfin septuagenarian Arnold Lipshitz croaked at the Board of Selectpersons sitting in front of him, stone-facedly enduring the barrage, "can't be this stupid. You just must be plain evil."

"Maybe fifty dollars a month doesn't

15

mean much to you," pear-shaped Daria Long said in her brusque, don't-you-know-common-sense-when-you-hear-it manner, "but for some of our folks it's going to be a choice between buying food and getting the garbage picked up."

Board member Casey Elliott couldn't stop himself. Picking nervously at his stringy black ponytail, he leaned into the microphone that craned over his position at the long, curved dais of the Board, the sweetness of his voice (high-fructose-corn-syrup sweetness, not quite Mexican Coke sweetness) almost masking the sharpness of his reply: "Well, it seems to me, the less food you buy, the less garbage we have to pick up. So wouldn't it be true that, seen just in this particular light, the problem kind of solves itself?"

The members of the Town of Gammage Board of Selectpersons, who had now endured a full evening of heated abuse in a woefully under-air-conditioned meeting room in late August, allowed themselves a guilty chuckle. Then, after having heard seventy-two citizens rail unanimously against the garbage tax, they did the inevitable: Declaring a municipal emergency (which bypassed the second-reading requirement and made their action take effect immediately), they passed the despised tax unanimously. During the hubbub of anger and frustration that now erupted in the cheap seats, the Board adjourned in memory of Elizabeth Gammage Stanton, the great-granddaughter of the town's founder, who had died the previous weekend of liver disease.

Over the customary coffee at T.G.I. Edy's, which stayed open late on Board nights, the Selectpersons rued their fate. "This was sinking pretty low," moaned Mayor Curtis Zorn. "I felt like shit sitting up there."

The eatery, filled with faux Art Deco fixtures and fake Tiffany windows, had been part of the nationwide TGIFriday's system, but when the chain pulled out, the new owners had had the money only to make a minimal change in the large sign out front. There was, in fact, no Edy.

Zorn, a thin, studious-looking man in his mid-thirties with dirty blond hair parted in the middle and long enough to be tucked behind his ears, had been elected mayor on a "good-government" platform — clean up the police department, improve the schools, plant new trees in the parks, the usual reform menu — and he was acutely embarrassed about devoting his first major effort

17

since the election to taxing Gammage's citizens for the privilege of not having their coffee grounds and grapefruit rinds and eggshells pile up in their sinks. Aside from words, he expressed that embarrassment by distractedly running his hands through his hair, as if a slightly neater personal appearance could compensate for the derelict state of his city.

"If you think you felt like shit tonight, wait till next month," Barbara Menzies said, beginning to devour her second chocolate doughnut of the night.

"What's next month?" Elliott asked, sipping a decaf.

"City manager wants a sewage tax," Menzies replied matter-of-factly. Menzies, known to her critics at Gammagegab.com, the online rump of the city's former daily newspaper, as "Barbara Menses," was a no-nonsense kind of woman, if you considered a seriously overweight lesbian with a mannish haircut to be lacking in nonsense. To the citizens of Gammage's Second District, though, she did what Selectpersons were supposed to do: get the bulbs in the streetlights replaced promptly, get last winter's potholes filled in before next winter started, get new pedestrian crossing stripes painted on the rare occasions when a street was

18

repaved. That, of course, was in the days when there was money in the city budget to do such things, in the days when the city's businesses had names like Target and Rite Aid and Exxon instead of Tergat and it Aid and XX, before the time of the garbage tax and the sewage tax and the excuse-me-for-living-here tax.

"Tell you one good thing," Casey Elliott confided while pulling the red scrunchy off his ponytail and letting his freak flag fly at the table, "we'd feel a heck of a lot worse if tonight's mess had been broadcast on WPUR." The Selectpersons chimed in with caffeinated agreement. WPUR, "Pure Radio," had been Gammage's local bastion of national culture, a public radio station nearly supporting itself by staging incessant bake sales, book sales, bike-a-thons, seed sales, wine auctions, movie screenings, potluck dinners, "Nights at the Symphony" (in Rochester), and every other kind of fund-raising event conceived by the non-profit mind. None of it was enough, given the town's reduced circumstances, to save the station, more recently known as "Poor Radio." It had pulled the plug on itself at the beginning of the year, selling its frequency to a Christian radio network that featured a format called "Hot Jesus Talk," and leaving the Board of Selectpersons meetings unbroadcast for the first time since the Korean War.

Its final day on the air constituted a kind of sour-grapes valedictory for WPUR. General Manager Earlene Hammond, a onetime New York City arts administrator (best remembered for her envelope-pushing melding of verse and gymnastics at the 92nd Street Y, "Poetry n Motion"), had taken the station's license from the public-school system and promised to turn the place into something people "would be proud to feel they need to support." On sign off day, Earlene wiped the slate clean of regularly scheduled programming in order to air a farewell forum on the topic "What Happened to Gammage?" Along with phone calls wondering "what happened to *Car Talk*?" citizens vented their anger over the hand that fate, and the economy, had dealt their town.

"It all started when we allowed the Goodway Tire plant to move to Quee-dad Juarez," one caller asserted. "See-you-dad," Earlene corrected. "Well, I'm sorry, they took our jobs, they can damn well put up with us pronouncing it however we like," the caller huffed. Then he asked whether he was getting a partial refund on his WPUR subscription. He was not, although he would be getting six monthly issues of *HELLO, LORD,* the program guide to the new format.

"Well, I blame former Mayor Ritter for letting the paper-bag mill move down to South Carolina," a woman caller groused. "Sure, it caused a lot of bad smells, and it killed a lot of fish, and I guess some folks didn't like that, but I suppose they like having a dead town better than some dead fish? We should have just let them bust the union like they wanted to, and we wouldn't be in this fix, and we'd still have *Prairie Home Companion* three times a weekend. We'll miss you." Earlene, deep into reading *The New York Review of Books* classifieds, grunted her appreciation.

"It was the shoe factory closing down that really did it," a young caller with a French-Canadian accent suggested. "That was the last straw on there. Maybe we should just get with it there, and all of us pack up and move to Malaysia, you know, follow the shoe factory. Maybe we need to be as mobile as the jobs are, maybe that's the future of capitalism there."

It was all true. Gammage had been savaged by downsizing, by outsourcing, by plant-closing. Michael Moore came in for a day, got a quick tour of the economic devastation, observed that the city's fate was "too damn depressing" for his next movie, and got out of town before dark.

Back at T.G.I. Edy's, as the coffee machine burped its last bit of brew, the city's leadership was formulating plans to bring Gammage back from over the brink.

2
GAMMAGE, NEW YORK
THE NEXT DAY

"Thank you for calling Wal-Mart."

"Yes," Mayor Curtis Zorn affirmed, as if to verify that he had not telephoned the mass merchandiser's corporate offices in error, "I'd like to —"

"We've recently changed our menu of options, so please listen closely," the surprisingly lifelike woman's voice advised. Curtis's own vocal equipment was a weedy tenor, something that sounded extruded rather than voluntarily produced to encourage human contact. So, while the machine enumerated the exciting possibilities of the new options menu at English-as-a-Second-Language pace, he rehearsed his approach, trying to pitch it somewhere in his vocal range that might possibly sound authoritative. "Hello, I'm Mayor Curtis Zorn, of Gammage, New York. Hello, I'm Curtis Zorn, Mayor of the City of Gammage, New York. It's actually a town, but . . . Hello,

23

I'm Mayor Curtis Zorn calling from the town I'm Mayor of, Gam—"

"Mr. Schwarzwelder's office."

"Yes, is he in?"

"One moment please, and I'll see."

One of life's mysteries, Zorn mused to himself, how a man's own secretary couldn't know off the top of her head whether or not he was "in." Curtis used the opportunity to re-familiarize himself with the music of Kenny G, which actually sounded just as good over the telephone as over the radio. Then, as the second song began, he unfolded a large map of Gammage and began reviewing the parcels of land suitable for a big-box superstore. There were a lot of them.

Mike Schwarzwelder, as it turned out, was in. His secretary had caught him just as he was on his way out the door to join other Wal-Mart executives for a two-day retreat at Burning Tree Country Club on the subject of "Retaining Our Connection to the Customer." The company had tried economizing during the recent speed bump in the economy by slashing travel expenses and running such seminars on closed-circuit satellite TV, but strangely enough, its executives preferred being lectured to after playing nine holes of golf or getting in a few laps in the pool. In any case, Mike was not in the mood for a long conversation.

"Mike Schwarzwelder," he barked in his pseudo-affable Illinois salesman's manner. He picked at the gap between his two upper front teeth with the business end of a number two pencil.

"Hey, Mike," Curtis began with road-company friendliness, "I'm Mayor Curtis Zorn of the Town of Gammage, in upstate New York, it's a beautiful community but, you know, we were just thinking about our retail base here in the community, and it occurred to us that something we could really use in town would be one of your great stores." Curtis paused for a gulp of oxygen.

It was interesting to Mike, a pitch this bald and pathetic. Usually, city officials, especially in the upper northeast, could be depended on to trot out the old malarkey about wiping out mom-and-pop stores, killing historic downtowns, and locating just outside municipal borders so as to deprive the poor city of vital sales-tax revenues, blah blah blah. As vice president for Corporate Real Estate, Schwarzwelder had heard variations on this theme played for as long as he'd been at Wal-Mart, and before then, in the same capacity at PetMax, a chain of pet-food superstores that were, like the dinosaurs, too huge to survive. But begging for a Wal-Mart didn't cut any more ice with Mike than pleading against one.

"Curtis — can I call you Curtis? — that's an extremely interesting proposition, a town that actually wants us to come in, and believe me, hearing you say that, your honor, is the next best thing to music to my ears."

Curtis couldn't help wondering what the next-best thing to music would actually be. Rushing water? Soft birdcalls? A gentle harp? — no, that *was* music. Mike wasn't speaking his words with the intention of having them examined closely. He was just filling time, operating in simple Silence Avoidance Mode, while he called up on his computer screen a program called Mart-Map that, drawing on proprietary databases of economic, demographic, and psycho-graphic information, graphically displayed which areas of the country did and didn't need additional Wal-Marts. One mouse click revealed that the entire sub-Canadian border region was, if anything, over served by the company, and that was the name of that tune. Before Curtis knew what hit him, he was on the list to receive a free videotape of Sam Walton's last Christmas message to his corporate family, and Mike was out the door, hell-bent for Burning Tree.

The computer was no kinder to Barbara Menzies than the phone was to Mayor Zorn. The clunky old Acer in the City Council office wheezed like an asthmatic spaniel and had a wine snob's disdain for the city's voltage-challenged electricity, but on a good day it still could handle simple e-mail traffic. "Two years ago," her outgoing message began, "I met you at the convention of gay and lesbian city council members in Eugene, Oregon. I had the short, salt-and-pepper hair and was wearing a caftan (and you kept joking that it was a muumuu — LOL!). Are you still involved in the field of telemarketing, because my city has just re-zoned an area of former warehouses, any one of which would make an absolutely perfect site for one of your 'boiler room'-type operations. Please let me know, as the Home Shopping Network people are coming in next week for a look-see at the spaces." The last sentence, of course, was a bald-faced lie.

The reply came a day later to womenzies@gammage.gov. "This is an automated reply. Thanks for your e-mail! At the moment, I'm incarcerated on trumped-up telephone fraud charges. But as soon as I'm released, I'll reply to your message personally."

There was one Gammage go-getter who'd actually succeeded in both going and getting: Dr. Roger Gardner, the superintendent of the Gammage School District. In a flush moment back in the '80s, Gammage had seceded from the County School District and almost immediately found itself floundering in enough red ink to print a year's worth of *USA Today*s. Dr. Gardner, as he insisted on being addressed, had taken the challenge and, as he liked to say, "turned the lemons into lemon meringue pie." So Gus Grissom Elementary and Christa McAuliffe High, the district's two schools, found themselves at what turned out to be the cutting edge of school finance: Dr. Gardner had cut exclusive deals for the schools' vending machines with Pepsi, he had made Puma the "official athletic equipment and activewear supplier to the Gammage School District," and half the textbooks in the two schools now bore discreet banners at the bottom of each page: "This adventure in learning made possible by your friends at MTV Networks."

Roger had his admirers, among them Dick Dirigian, the itinerant consultant who specialized in brokering such deals between cash-strapped schools and companies interested in the time-sharing of students' eyeballs. Dirigian discovered Gammage and its problems one summer while driving back from a short jaunt across the Canadian border to buy 222s, the codeine-laced aspirins legally sold over the counter in the Great White North ("The thing," he would say, "that makes the White North Great"). Now he used the school district and its "success story" as part of his traveling dog-and-pony show before dubious school boards up and down the Atlantic seaboard. Dr. Gardner had even been flown in, at Dick's expense, to try to apply the "closing touch" when Dirigian was pitching a New Jersey school district to make an exclusive deal for medical supplies with Johnson & Johnson, ultimately resulting in Secaucus High basketball team members wearing elbow sleeves and knee supports that looked perfectly normal except for the words "BAND-AID" printed in large red letters on the devices, letters readable (so the contract specified) from the fourteenth row.

There were those in Gammage who chafed at Dr. Gardner's insistence on the honorific (it was, in fact, a doctorate in televangelism from Bob Jones University, a relic from Roger's previous life; in one of his few self-deprecating remarks, he now referred to himself as "unborn again"), at his imperious formality (he wore a black three-piece suit every working day, complete with a key dangling from his vest pocket that looked for all the world like a Phi Beta Kappa key, but wasn't), at his utter conversion to the gospel of marketing. But the Selectpersons took Dr. Gardner to be what he claimed to be, "the man with the plan" for solving the town's malaise.

"What do you think, Dick?" Dr. Gardner had spread out a marketing prospectus for Gammage on the dining room table of his historic house, the northernmost point ever visited by Washington Irving. Dick Dirigian, whose life had been marginally enriched by his association with the doctor, squinted at the proposal, not so much from nearsightedness as from a good-faith attempt to act as if, seen through constricted eyeholes, the plan could look halfway sensible.

"See," Dirigian stroked his head carefully, so as not to disturb the contours of his graying comb-over, "an exclusive deal for school vending machines means something: Kids, impressionable, peer-influenced, not yet brand-loyal. An exclusive deal for vending machines at city facilities means what? The bus barn, city hall, the sewage plant?"

"Granted," Dr. Gardner conceded, speaking too loudly, almost as if he were addressing a conference of school administrators, "that's just a way to work concentrically outward from the familiar to the . . . the less familiar."

"I like the branded trash cans, conceptually, Dr. Gardner, I'm just trying to imagine who wants their logo on them."

"Same people who put their logos on the trash-collection trucks, I would think."

"Again, conceptually, I see where you're going with that, I'm just going through my mental Rolodex of clients."

"All right, well, the corporate name mowed into the lawns in city parks is more attractive, isn't it, Dick?"

"It's damned attractive, Rog— Dr. Gardner. It's a beautiful thing. Correct me if I'm wrong, as indicated in the rendering, it's basically readable only when viewed from directly above?"

"It's more readable from above, sure —"

"And there are no high-rise buildings adjoining any of the parks in Gammage, are there?"

"Well, not at the moment, no. That would

require a zoning change, but —"

"Okay, just want to be sure we're on the same page here."

Right now, Dick Dirigian was on the wrong side of the table. Not physically — the dark mahogany table in Dr. Gardner's dining room was as round as a crop circle. But it was contrary to Dick's whole existence to be the catcher, as opposed to the pitcher, to be the one who had to reject instead of the one facing — trying like hell to avoid — the rejection. It called for every ounce of smoothness Dick Dirigian could muster, and he had at his personal disposal great bulging tubs of smoothness.

If it wasn't in the genes, it was certainly in the years: the years spent as a legislative advocate at the New Jersey state capitol in Trenton (only outsiders called them "lobbyists"), as a drug-company detail man (he used to boast that he was responsible for more Zantac prescriptions than all the ex-wives in North America), and most recently as the guy who brought school districts and soft-drink giants onto Dick's favorite gathering spot, the same page. He was smoothness personified: In the subtle sheen of his Italian, broad-lapel, gunmetal gray suits; in the buttery baritone of his voice, which he soft-pedaled down to a reassuring purr; in the gaze of his blue-gray eyes that met but never penetrated; in the language that flattered while it extracted exactly what Dick Dirigian wanted. At the moment, he wanted more than anything not to be smoothly telling Dr. Roger Gardner that his plan for selling naming rights to the Gammage Water Filtration Plant was the marketing equivalent of pissing up a rope.

"Naming rights to a stadium, that I can do with half a frontal lobe whacked off, believe me, but naming rights to a big ugly building on the wrong side of town, of a town I might add that doesn't seem to have a right side, hey, *mi amigo,* sorry, no can do." Dick grinned, as if sharing a joke they both were in on.

Dr. Roger Gardner brushed some imaginary lint off the right sleeve of his suit jacket. "Okay, but this has got to be a natural, right? A product name or logo at the bottom or the top of each and every traffic ticket the town issues. You've got an exact, verifiable count of the eyeballs you reach, and if you're not reaching enough to satisfy the client, it's piece of cake time for the cop shop to up the ticket quota. That's candy from a baby, no?" Dr. Roger Gardner didn't personally think in clichés, but, from his self-ordained vantage point as the smartest man in Gammage, he found them a convenient way to ease communication with those for whom understanding came more slowly, such as everybody else.

"Here's what I think is at least doable," Dick oozed.

"Feasible," Dr. Gardner barked in stentorian tenor correction, unable to restrain the educator within.

"Feasible," Dick cooed, directing Dr. Gardner's attention to a proposal that called for painting sponsors' names over the double stripes in the middle of Gammage's principal streets, Elm, Maple, and Main. "I can anticipate one, what you might call a minor tweak," Dick added oleaginously, "which is that, contrary to the illustration, clients would probably want the thing painted with the product name facing drivers head-on, not lengthwise along the stripes."

"Really? But how would you keep from going outside the stripes onto the road itself?"

"Let them figure it out. That's why God made legal departments. But doing it your way, the only drivers who could read the name would be folks with great peripheral vision, or folks who turned their heads real fast to the left, which is a potential whiplash liability problem for the city, and, needless to say, none of us needs that right about now. Where's the john?"

Dr. Roger Gardner showed Dick Dirigian the way to the historic bathroom upstairs, the northernmost point at which Washington Irving is believed to have urinated. Then Dr. Gardner poured himself some instant iced tea and reflected on the possibility: He, the man the Selectpersons always scoffed at as an out-of-touch intellectual, would help shepherd the city out of its financial desert. Who'd be the egghead then?

3
WOWOSA,
CONNECTICUT
OCTOBER 1996

Tony Silotta had seen a lot of slot machines in his time, but never more of them gathered in one place than here, on the seemingly endless gaming floor of the Wowosa Casino: quarter slots, dollar slots, nickel slots, penny slots(!), progressive slots, million-dollar-payout slots, slots with a highly stylized portrait of Chief Rocking Bear — patriarch of the Wowosa Nation — on them, slots that put on a New Year's Eve-level video display every time you hit "play," slots that beeped like cell phones with Tourette's. Tony turned to his wife, Serena, and muttered, "They've got half the slots in the goddamn civilized world in here." She nodded her dutiful assent, knowing how the fact, and the observation, pained her man.

The Wowosa Casino was one the wonders of the modern world, a huge temple of gambling that blared its neon presence from within the sanctuary of the heavily wooded

Wowosa Reservation in the northern tip of Connecticut. Tony and Serena were on a busman's holiday, up from visiting her parents on Long Island, taking their first look at this phenomenon that burst on the gambling scene five years earlier and already boasted a "drop" that was the envy of every official of the gaming industry, an industry of which Tony was an executive avatar. Pained? He was practically having a myocardial infarction from the fucking rage he was feeling, as Don Nightswim, a one-thirty-second Wowosan who until two years ago called himself an African American and sold discount women's shoes at the Payless in downtown Hartford, showed the Silottas around the third floor, entirely devoted to roulette, as well as the blackjack wing, the craps pavilion, and the baccarat tower.

Not that Tony was any stranger to excess in the cause of stoking the desire to wager. He had worked himself up from being Tony "Loose Slots" Silotta, pit boss at Delmonico's, an old-time two-bit slot parlor on blue-collar Fremont Street in downtown Las Vegas to a position as that city's visionary statesman, partly through his swarthy good looks — the shiny black hair, the blazing white teeth that showed in a slightly feral smile, the tan that made George Hamilton's look sickly — but mainly by raising enough money to build the most outrageously excessive new hotels in an era of outrageous excess. His Hotel Katmandu, opened the previous year, offered a computer-generated Himalayan skyline out of every window and a twice-daily audience with the Dalai Lama for groups of twenty tourists willing to pony up a hundred dollars per head. None of them had yet objected that Katmandu was in Nepal while the Dalai Lama came from Tibet. Tony's previous venture, the Milano, featured a three-fifths-sized replica of the Duomo and slimmed-down versions of famous operas by a company from La Scala.

That was part of what so steamed him about Wowosa, as he sat with Serena in Chips, the utilitarian coffee shop tucked at the far end of the slots floor, after Don Nightswim had excused himself, nodding his goodbye and then catching his weighty headdress just as the feathers were about to take a dive into Tony's chicken in a pot. "Damnit, Reeny, they don't do doodley fuckin' squat except plug in the machines and count the money. No goddamn amenities, you know what I mean?" Serena nodded her sad agreement. "It's not a hotel, there's no entertainment, this rat-infested dump is the closest thing they have to a goddamn restaurant. . . . Their costs are zip fuckin' diddley zilch. It's just pure gaming, pure f-ing profit. And you know how they get away with it? Because they're fucking Indians," Tony sputtered, before remembering to look around to see if any Wowosas were minding the coffee shop. Of course, how could you tell? Judging by Don Nightswim, the W's looked just like average specimens who'd suddenly hit the jackpot by discovering they had a teaspoon, or an eyedropperful, of Indian blood in them. Some great-great-grandfather had taken an extremely temporary liking to some squaw, wham-bam-ugh, and now here these lucky bastards were, sitting on the biggest money pot since the Alaskan pipeline plopped on the tundra.

"Tone," Serena purred. "It's okay. What you're doing is reinventing the whole idea of a *gaming resort.* These people are just living in the past." Serena still had her good looks — great looks, if you counted the fake tits — that had originally attracted Tony to her when she was a covered dancer in *Oops!,* the naughty nude show at Tony's first big hotel, the Gold Rush. Full lips, blazing green eyes, red hair that still owed very little to the cosmetics counter at the Neiman

Marcus in Tony's upscale Vegas mall, Le Shoperie. She also retained her commitment to pleasing, calming, pacifying her guy, lest his legendary temper result in another scene like the one in Reno, where he fired every employee of the Gold Rush North and put the place into Chapter 11 over his profound dissatisfaction with the al dente-ness of the pastas turned out by Antonio's, the swank white-tablecloth restaurant he'd installed, against all knowledgeable advice, right next to the casino. Tony had his pride — huge, man-pleasing slabs of it.

"Reeny, what we're doing is fine, it's interesting, it's a novelty item. This is the bread and butter of the gaming industry right here. These fuckin' Seminoles or whatever they are don't pay any state taxes, they don't pay any federal taxes, they're splittin' the take with some Hoboken goombah, and that's it. It's so fucking sweet, this deal, it makes me want to puke blood."

"Tony, honey, don't puke blood, okay?"

"Okay. Just this once."

Tony was still seething a few hours later, arm-dancing his anger on the steering wheel of his rented Lexus, cruise-controlled speeding across the Connecticut–New York border toward his in-laws' vacation home near Lake Pleasant. It was a little early in the fall for the leaf peepers to be at full strength, but the two-lane state highway still had its share of Buicks creeping along while drivers and passengers pointed and oohed and ahhed at the occasional flaming maple.

This behavior didn't significantly improve Tony's disposition. While Serena sat watching the trees flash past her, Tony was yelling into the earpiece-and-microphone attachment connected to his cell phone, hitting manual override on the cruise control just long enough to roar into the oncoming lane, leaving a peeper in his dust.

"Leon, please, don't waste my time telling me what I know. I know we got *our* legislature wired, I'm talking about Congress. Nobody else can put a rein on this redskin racket. Indian bingo. Indian poker machines. Indian casinos. These so-called natives are getting away with murder. I'm telling you, Leon, if our trade association can't somehow get a handle on this shit, the only way your law firm or my company is gonna make any money is if we corner the market in fucking buckskin. GET OUT OF THE GODDAMN ROAD, YOU MORON!"

Tony punctuated this last instruction with a medley of fine honking. The overloaded lime green Oldsmobile Cutlass ahead of him, which looked as if it were in fact his father's Oldsmobile, waddled over to the shoulder, and Tony roared by.

At the other end of the line, patiently listening to Tony vent while he checked his stock portfolio on Ameritrade, was Leon Wendelkind, an all-purpose fixer for the Silotta empire. It was Leon, skilled in the law as well as the more arcane crafts of the profession, who had convinced the Nevada Water Resources Board, nominally concerned about husbanding scarce resources in a desert environment, that it was not wasteful to let Tony build a replica of Niagara Falls at his forthcoming new venture, the Waterworld Hotel. Leon had negotiated the naming rights for the same project with Kevin Costner's company (it was amazing how much money people could demand for a tie-in to a flop). Leon had even convinced the board to allow the mini-Niagara not to recirculate its water, but to suck in a new supply every hour. He could work wonders, Leon Wendelkind could, but even he didn't think he could put the Indians out of business. He knew Tony well enough not to share that information with him at the moment, out of concern for the welfare of the other drivers on State Route 8.

"Tony, Tony, stop yelling for one minute and listen to me, okay?" Leon finally urged, using his "sweet-reason" voice. Like all good lawyers, Wendelkind had at his disposal a variety of vocal modes, stops on the organ of loquacity. The ability to shift in and out of the appropriate mode was one of those arcane skills of which he was most proud. "I know a guy in D.C., let me give him a call. I got him out of a drunk-driving thing one time, he may decide to start feeling grateful. Maybe I can find some place on the Native American windpipe where we can place a well-chosen finger or two."

4
WASHINGTON, D.C.
FALL 1996

Vince Winstanley was a lifer. About everything. He'd had a crew cut since the Top 40
included songs by The Crew Cuts, and he'd
stuck with it, through thick and thin — literally. He'd had his first taste of government
work as a legislative intern in Sacramento,
part of a corps of eager young grad students
and draft dodgers sucked into the lawmak-
ing maw when the then-Speaker of the
California State Assembly decided that what
would make the legislative process less like
the sausage-making process (to which it was
always being compared) was professional-
ization — as if the main problem with either
business was excessive amateurism. Now,
decades later, Vince enjoyed GS-18 status
in the federal government, which meant he
could be dismissed from employment only
in the event of a prolonged thermonuclear
conflict.

He was still married to Eileen, his first

and only wife, an arts administrator, who had retained her frosted-blond flip and girlish giggle while picking up a flair for Italian cooking. They entertained their peers, other government lifers, and members of the lobbyist class who were confident enough to waste evenings with people who had neither choice committee assignments in Congress nor cable talk shows. They bicycled along the C&O Canal, they attended the few European movies that came to Washington, they went to Umbria every other summer, and they rarely looked back at their choice to go childless. It was a variety of happiness.

Inside the Interior Department, Vince had earned a reputation as a firefighter. When allegations surfaced that Yellowstone's primary tourist attraction, Old Faithful, was now spouting with a serious lack of fidelity because of slant oil drilling on the national park's southeastern border, Vince had volunteered to take on the mess. Within ten months, the geyser was back on schedule and Rapier Oil Corporation was none the poorer. When Alaskan Inuits angrily protested that the footprint of the DIRECTV satellite did not include the forty-ninth state, thereby launching anti-indigenous-peoples discrimination onto a new technological frontier, Winstanley had applied gentle pressure on the DIRECTV folks to give their satellite a slight northward nudge. Vince liked to believe that he specialized in win-win solutions.

Perhaps, he thought, he wouldn't have worked so hard to earn that reputation had he known what it would win *him:* a deputy-assistant secretaryship at the Bureau of Indian Affairs. BIA was to the Interior Department what UPN was to television networks. It was the Geo Metro of government agencies, maybe even the Yugo. It was the place where your career went to curl up and die. BIA officials often found themselves hearing about Interior Department office parties after the fact, not even bothering to wonder why they hadn't been invited. Indian Affairs was the only agency in official Washington that still had its phone calls answered by a live operator, who bravely recited the "our menu has recently changed" telephone-tree script, despite the fact that there was no menu, and no tree. The night Vince found out about the BIA "promotion," Eileen had fixed him an elegant celebratory repast — pasta shells with tricolor peppers, veal with artichokes, a zucchini-blossom soufflé — and he poked at it as sullenly as a Siamese eat confronted with last week's Whiskas.

The agency's lowly status, of course, was to some extent a reflection on its constituency, the Native Americans whom, over the past century, it had, to be richly euphemistic, "served." Vince approached the bureaucratic life with a dry if not desiccated amusement, and he had often enlivened slow summer afternoons at the Interior library, catching up on the minefields, mishaps, and malefactions that BIA had accumulated.

There had been the policy of "termination," an attempt to redirect Indians off the reservations and into the mainstream. Ill-prepared for the transition by the very agency that was pushing it, the Native Americans who allowed themselves to be "terminated" often suffered the sociological equivalent of the bends.

Mineral rights to the reservations had long since been sold off by the BIA, which had somehow forgotten to keep records of the transactions so it might pass the income on to the tribes that still held title to the land. After nearly a century, this situation was now spawning lawsuits whose possible payouts could make an anti-tobacco litigator feel light-headed.

And there was the little unsolved matter of the unrecognized tribes, 250 groups of Native Americans who enjoyed neither tribal sovereignty nor the alloyed pleasures of reservation life because the federal government had never signed treaties with them. About a hundred such groupings were actively seeking recognition, the process was proceeding at a pace that glaciers and snails would envy, and that was the indigestible bureaucratic morsel that had been served up to Vince Winstanley. Take over the Branch of Acknowledgment and Research, his boss, Hap Matthews, had told him, and do whatever you can to get these tribes out of our hair.

Gray in every way — voice, clothes, hair, demeanor — Hap was so close to retirement age that he could taste the Dentu-Creme, and he wanted this little matter resolved before any staffer working for any member of Congress could muster interest in the question of tribal acknowledgment. Once Congress got its nose under the tent, you had questions to answer, forms to fill out, hearings to attend. To Hap's way of thinking, it was as if high-ranking, hard-working government officials could be reduced to the status of — he inwardly grimaced to think about it — Indians themselves. Ugh.

And the solution, he told Vince, was so easy. "Look," he said over croissants and lattes at Starbucks, the better not to be overheard, "acknowledgment is just like certification, right?" Vince, who was known inside the Department as much for his Boy Scout dedication to doing the Right Thing as for his droll acceptance of others' different value systems, nodded uncertainly.

"We certify that the Hanford site is an adequate place to store high-level nuclear waste. Why? *Because there's no other place to put the stuff.* We certify that Mexico is our ally in the War on Drugs, because if we don't, the drug lords who run that godforsaken, piece-of-shit excuse for a country will start picking off our DEA officers like skeet on a Sunday. So, how much skin is it off whose ass if we certify or acknowledge these tribes as Indians before our so-called panel of experts has finished reading every last piece of carved bark on the subject, you know what I'm saying?"

So Vince set up shop in a spacious office in the Ronald Reagan Building, the largest civilian federal office block ever constructed. It was built as a monument to the Republican Party's champion of small government,

49

and forty thousand small governments would fit nicely inside it. Vince hung his Ansel Adams silver-chrome photographs of Mount Shasta and Monument Valley and Oak Creek Canyon on the walls, he put his Navajo rugs on the floor, and he sent out a memo setting a deadline for the BIA's historians, geneologists, and anthropologists to decide on the pending application of North Dakota's would-be Little Shell tribe: before the end of the fiscal year. Based on the agency's recent track record, one tribal acknowledgment in ten months would qualify as heart-pounding speed.

5
OUTSIDE GAMMAGE, NEW YORK
OCTOBER 1996

"And what brings you to Lake Pleasant?" Dick Dirigian asked, exuding charm the way a department-store cologne counter exudes musk. The target of his question was a model-thin redhead whom he'd encountered moments ago at the bar of The Emerald, the only cocktail lounge/pub/dive on the lake's south shore. Dick had driven up from Gammage to get some fishing done before heading on to Buffalo, where he hoped to put the city's schools and the Frito-Lay people on the same page. With his salesman's instinct for "the close," Dick let no more than milliseconds elapse before he struck up what he was sure sounded like friendly conversation.

"Oh, we're here visiting my parents," the redhead answered, sipping her Semillon Blanc with bus-and-truck nonchalance.

"So you're married," Dick suggested.

"I'm so married, it's ridiculous."

"Anybody I should know?"

"You spend much time in Vegas?"

Vegas had so much gambling money streaming out of its every pore that its schools could actually support themselves, with no need for the ministrations of a Dick Dirigian. In Las Vegas, the school district still retained the right to decide what beverages were sold on its campuses. It struck Dick as a primitive vestige of a time long gone.

"Not since they tore down the Sands. See, the Copa Room, now *that* was a showroom. Classy. Elegant. Even if you were sitting there watching some piece of crap Jim Nabors show, it always felt like Sinatra just might drop in and lay a few tunes in your lap. But now it's all changed, you know, it's a, it's just a theme park. Some of the newer places, like the MGM, they're just aircraft hangars with maître d's. Excuse me, I hope your husband doesn't run the MGM?"

"Not hardly. He wouldn't even let me dance there. He said he spent more money building my tits than Kirk Kerkorian did building that whole dump. He was kidding, of course."

"Of course."

Dick now allowed himself a second, more

appraising, glance at the construction project in question. Somebody, he thought, got his money's worth.

It was a thought interrupted. Dick's field of vision suddenly went all sparkly while a dull but decidedly attention-getting pain pulsed along the perimeter of his left eye socket. It was, he mused, as the sparkly field became a panorama of black velvet, almost as if someone had come up from behind and punched him hard in the eye. So with all this black velvet, he wondered with the clarity of the newly brain-dead, why hadn't anybody bothered to paint some clowns?

Noneonta Valley Hospital didn't really have an emergency wing anymore. After the last round of budget cuts, doctors in the surrounding three counties had signed a pledge to not be on call. The emergency entrance was now fortified, blocked off with a phalanx of orange traffic cones and a wall of Jersey barricades that just served to make the place look as if the emergencies had moved outside for the night. One vestige of the hospital's flush days remained: a marquee stood outside the main entrance, the kind that proclaim in front of suburban high schools, "Welcome, Romans" or "Pre-reg this Friday. *Grease* next weekend."

Noneonta Valley's sign still carried the proud message, under the facility's name: "Putting the 'hospitality' back in 'hospital.' "

The owner of The Emerald knew one of the staff doctors, so both Dick Dirigian and Tony Silotta were admitted, even though it was half past midnight when the Chevy van carrying the two gladiators pulled up to the hospital's front door. As the gurneys were being wheeled through Receiving (closed), past Insurance (closed), and into a couple of available examination rooms, Dick couldn't help himself: He struck up a conversation with Tony.

" 'Loose Slots,' that's a hell of a nickname they pinned on you."

"It beats 'Three Fingers'."

"You got me there. So, like they say in jail, what are you in for?"

"Shortly after I decked your sorry ass, the owner of the bar sucker punched me from behind for starting a commotion. That fucking excuse for a bar, a good commotion is exactly what they need."

"So you're what's-her-name's husband?"

"Yeah, that's right. I saw you staring at her boobs. I own those."

"Hey, no harm in looking."

"You just proved that wrong."

"I guess I did."

Dick was being gregarious, and apologetic, with a guy who had socked him in the eye for noticing what he, the guy, had paid big money to *get people to notice.* The admitting physician was about to examine Dick when Tony flashed his $10,000-for-whitening-and-straightening smile and slipped the doctor a couple of C-notes from underneath his sheet. In the click of a gurney's wheels, Dick found himself in an empty examination room, conducting a one-eyed appraisal of a two-year-old wall calendar and some Canadian medical magazines.

Dick ended up needing six stitches around the eye socket, and Tony got a couple of dozen for the spot where his forehead had collided with a Super Bowl ring The Emerald's owner had bought on eBay. The admitting physician was not too fatigued from the thirty-six-hour shift he was pulling as part of his residency to advise his late-night patients that the hospital's kitchen had just been cited by the Health Department, and not in a good way. So Dick and Tony each decided that he'd partaken sufficiently of the once-famous hospitality. Dick's goofy gregariousness now paid a dividend; Tony offered Serena's services to drive them back to The Emerald, where Dick's car was still parked. Along the way, Dick Dirigian started to figure out his companions.

For one thing, Tony now seemed exceptionally amorous toward Serena, almost making the champagne-colored Lexus lurch through the early dawn each time he licked the stocking on her accelerator leg. At times, it seemed to Dick that the amorousness, if not being performed for his benefit, was at least stimulated by his presence in the back-seat.

"You strapped in there, Dick?" Tony asked at one point. "Because I don't want any interference up here." Serena just kept on driving.

At other moments, Tony relaxed, his passion sated for the time being. That's when his anger started boiling up, perhaps also for Dick's benefit. "Dick, let me ask you a question: You ever been to the Wowosa Casino?"

Dick, who prided himself on his salesman's sense of the answer his questioner wanted to hear, chose wrong. "It's amazing, Tony. Absolutely mind-boggling place. Why, you got a piece of that action, too?"

"Are you out of your fucking mind? Reeny, stop the car."

"But, Tone —"

Tony placed a hand on her right shoulder that seemed to chill every part of her body, except for the artificial breasts. Serena brought the luxury vehicle to an abrupt stop on the shoulder. Tony sat in the passenger seat, shaking his head, trying to suppress the surplus emotion welling up inside him.

"I am going . . . to get that . . . place closed down . . . if it's . . . the last thing I do on this earth."

Dick felt himself shifting into reverse so fast that it could have given him whiplash if he were a passenger in his own head. "And a good thing, too, Tony, that place is a menace. What is it, exactly, that agitates you, the gambling, the pollution, the —"

"It's the Indians, Mr. Dirigian," Serena answered while Tony was still inhaling for the verbal explosion he planned to detonate. It was the first time Serena had talked to Dick Dirigian since they sat together in The Emerald. The thought made Dick's eye socket throb.

"Ah, well, they're getting away with murder, those Indians," Dick said agreeably. He saw the rage drain from Tony's face, and he got a little less tense. Maybe he'd actually be back in his own car before any more harm came to his person.

Tony gave Serena a signal, she started the

car up, and the Lexus pulled back onto the highway. After a moment, Tony turned around. "You know, Dick," Tony said gently, "a two thousand dollar investment in a halfway decent weave and you could kiss that comb-over crap good-bye."

A few miles down the road, Tony settled into a reflective mood. That was the mood in which he told his life story to total strangers, rehearsing the saga for the book deal he knew in his heart he was *this* close to making with one of the big houses. "My dad," he said as Dick fought off the wooziness of his pain medication, "was from Sicily, see. He moves down to South Africa because, hey, in those days, if you're from southern Europe, it was easier to get into than America, and a cheaper trip than Australia."

"Mmm, I've heard that place is beautiful," Dick said, losing the fight with dreaminess momentarily.

"What place?" Tony asked with a hint of menace.

"Australia. Supposed to be the best diving on the —"

"So Evangelino — that's his name — right?, that's strike one right there, he figures out that the one thing a white guy

58

can do in South Africa that makes lots of money and keeps you out of, let's say, the line of fire, is open a casino in one of the Bantustans."

"I hear they're beautiful, too," said Dick, trying so very hard to please.

"They're okay. They're like Nevada without the water. But the deal is, they're like little fake countries that are totally controlled by the government. So you're splitting the take with the guys who regulate you. On top of taxes. That's the world I grew up in. So you can imagine, when I get to be in my early twenties, and I'm rebellious as hell, I'm eating American, I'm talking American, and I'm driving my dad crazy with, 'Why the hell are you putting up with skimming by the fucking government?' Finally, one day, he's exhausted, trying to convince Vic Fucking Damone to come down and play a weekend in the showroom, he just turns to me and says, 'Okay, Mr. Big Shot, why don't you go to America and leave me the fuck alone.' "

"I am in America," Dick pointed out helpfully.

"Next time I talked to Evangelino, I owned half of Vegas, and he was in a hospital bed reciting the alphabet backwards in Italian. Reeny, pull over at the next rest stop.

Let's pump some coffee into our friend here before letting him loose."

6
GAMMAGE, NEW YORK
LATE OCTOBER 1996

"Now this is the same sort of thing you people are always doing, so I really shouldn't be surprised, but still it's just so sad, and that doesn't make it any better for those of us who still pay attention to you people, in case you didn't think any of us do."

Lucy Striker was standing at the podium at the Board of Selectpersons meeting in her usual pose — a faded manila folder stuffed full of news clippings, official reports, and printed-out e-mail advisories under her left arm, her right arm holding on to the podium's front lip as if it gave her the energy to soldier on, if not the will to live. Her speaking voice could be charitably described as a drone that spent a lot of prep time in her nose, and her physical appearance revealed a refreshing lack of vanity. The garment she wore would be called a housedress if she didn't wear it outside the house, and her chin-length gray-brown hair looked as if it hadn't been washed since the Cubs won the World Series. But she cared about her community, as she knew too few of her neighbors did. If that caring had curdled to a dark suspicion of the forces arrayed against her on virtually every issue that came before the Board, Lucy knew that was the price of being a Concerned Citizen. At least in her presentations at the podium, her face seemed fixed in a perpetual scowl of scolding disappointment.

Lucy attended every meeting of the Selectpersons, submitted a chit to speak on every issue, and for her efforts won the more or less passive inattention of every member of the Board. She saw herself as a courageous citizens' watchdog; the city dads and moms saw her as an unavoidable, pestilential nuisance. All of them were correct.

Her chief legacy, the monument to her persistence if not her persuasiveness, was a rule change, reducing from three minutes to two minutes the amount of time a citizen could speak before the Board if said citizen had already spoken before the Board that evening. Lucy called it a "bill of attainder." The Board majority, unanimous in this particular case, called it common sense. All of them were correct.

Tonight Lucy's fusillade of outrage was

aimed at a proposal by Dr. Roger Gardner. Seeing the budget ax swinging inexorably toward his district, suffering from a severe cost overrun on a new magnet school built over a recently discovered vein of methane, he had preemptively put forward what he called a "bold new plan to put the city's fiscal feet on firm flooring." (Dr. Gardner was a believer in the power of alliteration.) The plan was to build on other governments' experiences in privatizing their jails and sanitation operations. "They make money and they run the facilities much more efficiently. That's what we call a win-win situation," Dr. Gardner told the Selectpersons. Mayor Curtis Zorn swiveled his big leather armchair sideways from the Board's horseshoe dais and whispered to Barbara Menzies, "Who's we?" Dr. Gardner's plan, simple and elegant, was to privatize the city's thoroughfares — sell its streets, roads, avenues, lanes, circles, crescents, drives, alleys, and its one boulevard to the highest bidder and then sit back and let the money roll in while the lucky bidder took up the burden of maintenance, pothole repair, snow removal, painting new lane dividers, and the like.

"Hey, but wait a second, Dr. Gardner," Curtis interposed as Roger began placing large placards with happy, four-color cash-flow projections on easels around the board-room. "Does this mean the citizens of this community are going to have to pay for the privilege of using their own streets? That doesn't sound very —"

"They do, anyway, in the form of taxes. There's no free lunch, as you well know, Mr. Zorn." Dr. Gardner had an orator's way of talking, so even as he semicircled the room, unveiling his optimistic charts, his unamplified bark of a voice filled the chamber. He also had a way of making the questioner feel like someone who was in imminent danger of flunking dumbbell English. That skill, combined with his vaulting ambition, had propelled him out of the classroom, where he taught tenth-grade social studies to teenagers whose resentment level was not lessened by his condescension, and into the world of administration.

Lucy proceeded through her standard two-minute plainsong of anger, a stream of semi-consciousness narrative about the malevolence of privatization, the bankruptcy of civic imagination, and — whatever topic that was to follow was drowned out by the harsh ring of the "time's-up" bell (a cheap egg timer, a Christmas gift to the city from the Selectpersons) and by Mayor Curtis Zorn's gavel. She was followed to the podium by about a dozen residents, some bewildered, some outraged by Dr. Roger Gardner's audacious notion.

Casey Elliott, his greasy ponytail adorned for the meeting with a green scrunchy (more precisely, a Green scrunchy, a party favor from a recent Green Party rally), took over when the time for public comments had expired. "So just explain to me how would this work, exactly. Would we sell all the streets to, like, one company, like a cable TV franchise?" These last words set off a vigorous round of booing in the room, since Gammage Cable, one of the few local outfits not yet gobbled up by the giants in the late-'90s cable consolidation, was notorious for its bounteous array of lousy pictures and for its still lousier customer service — even considering that the bar in the industry had been set remarkably low.

"That's one model," Dr. Gardner responded, his voice climbing easily over the catcalls, "and, judging by the response here tonight, probably not the most popular one." The hint of a smile on Dr. Roger Gardner's lips signaled to savvy insiders that they were being treated to just a sliver of the man's vaunted wit. "But we could divide the thoroughfares into packages, bid each one off to a different company, and the ones that charge the least for access, or do the best job of keeping them clean and nice, will get the most traffic. People who want a faster drive may end up paying more for that privilege, as they probably should."

Barbara Menzies seemed to sum up the feelings of the Board at the end of yet another tumultuous meeting when she scrunched up what keen observers might recognize as her shoulders, leaned toward her microphone, and murmured glumly, "With all due respect to Dr. Gardner, and with a great appreciation for all the hard work that he so obviously put into these wonderful charts, I really think that the answer to our money crisis in this community has yet to be found."

"No shit," Dr. Roger Gardner whispered to no one in particular.

7
WASHINGTON, D.C.
EARLY NOVEMBER
1996

"Be Nice or Leave." It seemed to Vince Winstanley to be some sort of mantra. At least it showed up in some corner of every one of the painted tin ceiling squares that comprised the "outsider art" exhibit his wife, Eileen, had convinced him to attend after a long Tuesday of trying to push the toothpaste of Indian tribe recognition out through the tube of Indian Affairs. The outsider artist, who signed himself "Dr. Bob," painted on the squares, reclaimed from old office buildings being leveled. He painted scenes of rural honky-tonks, road-houses tucked deep into swampy Southern woodlands, the kind of places that had stopped existing precisely when the office buildings now being demolished in Memphis, Charlotte, and Atlanta were first going up. Eileen thought it would make a fine traveling exhibit for funding by Philip Morris or Monsanto, or some other company in desperate need of funkifying its image. Vince thought he could be home watching the kickoff of Shark Week on the Discovery Channel.

"You know," Eileen said in a moment of inspiration as they stood in front of Riverfront Cafe #2, "this would be a great show to put on the Internet, and the sponsorship money would be much easier to assemble."

"I suppose," Vince mused, "but how would you scan pressed squares of tin into a computer?"

Eileen waved her digital still camera at Vince with a lovingly sardonic grin, sympathizing with an overstressed man who had momentarily lost the use of part of his frontal lobe. As Vince nodded in self-mocking acknowledgment, his cell phone went off, playing in tinkly electronic monophony the theme from the first movement of Beethoven's Symphony #8. Vince plugged the headset attachment (essential, he knew, for preventing brain tumors) into his right ear and hit the "talk" button on the tiny device. "Winstanley," he whispered, concerned that he was upsetting his fellow gallery-goers.

"Vince," boomed the voice at the other end, "Leon Wendelkind. Your office told me you were reachable there. How are you? How's your driving?"

"It's fine, Leon, and I'm fine, too." Leon was a reminder to Vince of a very unhappy episode from seven years back. Eileen and he had been at a gala Washington dinner, celebrating his twentieth anniversary at the government trough; he had pooh-poohed her idea of hiring a limo for the night, and then, as he drove home, later than he usually stayed up and with an after-dinner cognac sloshing around on top of the vittles, a D.C. cop with too little to do had stopped his car and breath-tested him. Vince was sure he was sober but tired. The cop was sure he was drunk. The next morning, Leon had been brought in, not so much to mediate that debate as to wave his magic wand and make the whole incident go away before it became the first stain on Vince's pristine employment record.

It had been bad enough to need Leon in such a circumstance. The experience became worse the more time Vince spent talking to his attorney about the details of making the matter disappear. Wendelkind had an odd habit of telling people unpleasant facts (like "you're going to have to go down to this lab in Virginia and have a baseline urine test, just in case we get lucky and you're naturally high in blood alcohol") and finishing the thought with a jaunty "Okay?" Vince, normally the mildest-mannered of men, more than once during the brief relationship had to fight off the urge to yell back at Leon, "No, as a matter of fact it's not okay. None of this is okay. *How in your wildest dreams could you imagine that any of this is anything remotely resembling okay?*"

Now here was Leon resurfacing like poorly painted-over linoleum. This was not what Vince needed. "Mind if we meet for coffee somewhere in the neighborhood tonight? I've got something I need to ask you, okay? How about Reds, that's just a couple blocks over on M."

Before Vince could muster an answer, the line went dead.

Reds was one of the hottest restaurants in turn-of-the-century Washington. Like most other fashions, Retro-Soviet Chic had come late to the nation's capital, but it came with a vengeance. Rising in the midst of the tony Dupont Circle neighborhood was a thick slab of brutal Stalinist architecture. Its cheap concrete walls (the same concrete, according to the press release, used in the Chernobyl containment vessels) were lined with Socialist Realist murals of The Workers

Triumphant. Its flaked Formica tables were covered with plates of beef Stroganoff and chicken Kiev and more things done with potatoes than the Idaho Agricultural Commission had ever dreamed of. On the front of the menus was the iconic black-and-white photograph of Nikita Khrushchev banging his shoe on the dais during his speech at the U.N. in the late 1950s. From his mouth came a cartoon-like speech balloon, containing the restaurant's jaunty slogan: "We will bury you — with blinis!"

Wendelkind was one of the small band of what the newspapers were required to call "high-powered Washington lawyers" who maintained roughly equivalent links to both Republicans and Democrats. It wasn't a matter of lacking an ideology; he liked to explain to younger attorneys coming into the firm, just the simple precaution of keeping the business flowing no matter who happened to win an election. Still in his forties but looking even younger thanks to those discreet trips West every couple of years to doctors recommended by middle-aged TV newsman friends, Wendelkind maintained the allegiance of im- portant Washingtonians by inducing his model-thin wife, Rachel, to hold what were agreed to be the capital's most interesting dinner parties since Arianna Huffington had left town. He also maintained a ready supply of Wizards tickets.

Eileen Winstanley had stayed back at the gallery to find out just how cheaply Dr. Bob's oeuvre could be cyber-mounted, so Vince took a table with Leon and waited for what he knew in his gut would be an unpleasant surprise, okay? Leon ordered the diet blinis (no caviar, no sour cream, no butter), Vince opted for the cold borscht, and while their waiter — who wore an ill-fitting dark gray Gromyko suit and introduced himself as "Comrade Dylan" — brought the bread, Leon gently dropped the hammer.

"What would it take to make the continued operation of the Wowosa Casino a lot more trouble than it's worth?"

Vince whistled a descending scale, ran his hands across his crew cut, and took a piece of bread. "Before I answer your question, is it just me, or did Comrade Dylan forget to bring us butter?"

"It's a Soviet-style restaurant. All they've got is this white margarine."

"Ah. Well, Leon, you couldn't be making that particular inquiry at a worse time. I don't know whether you saw the hearing this week on C-SPAN 2 —"

"Can I tell you something, Vince? My building doesn't get C-SPAN 2, and C-SPAN 1 alternates with the Food Network at night, so —"

"It was a hearing at the Senate Subcommittee on Indian Affairs. They're pushing us pretty hard."

"Hey, it's the Senate, they're always pushing somebody. That's a big part of their job description."

"Well, the chairman sent some unmistakable smoke signals that if we don't want to be zeroed out come appropriation time next year, we'd better become a much more Indian-friendly type of operation, and do it right away. That's become my mandate, seriously. I mean, if some Native Americans want casinos, they're going to get casinos. If they want their trust fund moneys repaid with compound interest, they're going to get that. Actually, *that* we owe them, but now they're actually going to get it. Leon, here's how bad it is: We're getting so much pressure from the Hill to speed up the acknowledg- ment of the 'forgotten tribes' that right about now you could get certified as an Indian."

"Tempting, but I think my rabbi would object."

Comrade Dylan approached the table at this point. "Who's got the potato beer?"

8
UPSTATE NEW YORK
EARLY NOVEMBER
1996

Dick Dirigian had to call the people in Buffalo and take a rain check. "That is what you folks call it, isn't it, because, my God, you guys must be so used to bad weather, I'd imagine you wouldn't have anything but snow checks, or maybe just blizzard checks." One of the things about being compulsively amiable is that you could never just say something simple, you had to keep embellishing it with an unstoppable flow of what you hoped didn't sound like desperate attempts at attention retention.

Dick's time was ceasing to be his own. Tony Silotta had invited him up to the lake, where Tony's in-laws had a place, and Dick got the distinct impression that you don't thank Tony very kindly and turn down his invitations. Even a very, very kindly thanking was probably unwise. So Dick was at the lake, as he told the people in Buffalo, for his health. Literally.

The afternoon was crisp. Actually, it was brisk. Freezing was more like it, but Tony, Serena, and Dick weren't there to putter around indoors, Tony had announced, so they were sitting on the deck, fishing lines lazily poking into the lake, bundled up in parkas and, in Serena's case, a black fox fur jacket. Dick was explaining the ins and outs of his business to a fascinated Tony, while Serena sorted through the three most recent issues of *Allure.*

"So the school lets you have an exclusive deal to sell them soft drinks why again?" Tony probed.

"Because the district or the city government can't or won't raise taxes, and this is the school's best bet at generating a new revenue stream," Dick answered. "You know, the cola companies love to market to kids, the kids love to drink cola, it's like a marriage made in sugar heaven. Listen, I didn't invent this business, I just happen to be one of the kings of it."

"No, I know, I'm just thinking. What else could you make an exclusive deal with schools for?" The idea of an exclusive deal, with anybody, for anything, twinkled in Tony's mind like a desert sky at midnight.

"Well, let's see . . ." Dick couldn't decide whether Tony was planning to go into a partnership deal with him or pumping him for data before dumping his lifeless corpse into the lake.

"Books?"

"That's already an exclusive, my friend, usually through the state. That's major-league lobbying business, that is. What I do doesn't involve nearly that much heavy lifting. Just a lunch with a school principal — at worst dinner with a district superintendent — show 'em the figures on what a Coke or a Pepsi will pay them, watch their eyes get big as basketball hoops, and while they're still in mid-drool, bam!, I'm outta there with a signed contract before you can say non-stop flight." Dick immediately regretted the Emeril reference, but Tony ignored it, more interested in pushing the exclusivity envelope.

"Gym equipment? Shorts, athletic supporters, cups —"

"Nike's already there. Adidas is playing serious catchup ball. They don't use brokers like me, they have a shitload of washed-up ex-athletes on the payroll. You want to hold Reggie Williams's hand, you're welcome to it, brother."

"Who the f—"

Tony's expletive was interrupted by the chirping of his cell phone, playing the world's tinkliest version of "New York, New York." He shot a glance at the caller ID number flashing on the screen, then snuggled the instrument against his right ear. "Yeah. Talk to me, Leon." While Tony listened, nodding sullenly, Dick Dirigian concentrated on looking at the lake, knowing that any glances he cast at Serena's breastworks might endanger his good eye socket. But, thanks to the superior peripheral vision that he'd always enjoyed, Dick did notice that Mrs. Silotta was now painting her toenails cobalt blue.

Even with the painting, and the nippy breeze, and the lively editorial tone of the *Allure* articles, Serena was having a hard time staying awake. These were the dead times — afternoons. Her body clock had been factory set for the lifestyle of a Vegas covered dancer (the highest-ranking showgirl in the town's hierarchy, above dancing nudes and nudes), and the change to married life and early retirement from the stage had done nothing to readjust her internal TAG Heuer. She perked up for a moment when the "Habañera" from *Carmen* indicated that someone was calling Dick's cell phone. But almost instantly she settled into a comfortable hazy reverie as Tony's and

Dick's voices intertwined, their mutually private conversations enveloping her.

Tony: "He said the Indians got carte rouge? What the hell does that mean?"

Dick: "Roger, I've just been going over this with my friend here. He's — he's my friend."

"Sure I appreciate wordplay, Leon, I'd love to devote an entire showroom to it, for Chrissake, unfortunately Oscar Fucking Wilde died a hundred years ago. So where does that leave us?"

"Gum, what about selling gum in the classrooms? I'm sure we could get some serious money from the Wrigley's people for an exclusive. They have't played in this ballgame yet, I could squeeze their nuts good and hard."

"You know, Leon? This is the first time in my life I've ever thought I'd rather not be Italian. Jesus, ain't that a kick in the gazon-gas."

"So you *change* the rules. What's so wrong about kids chewing gum in class, anyway? They're grinding away at some fine spearmint product, maybe they're too preoccupied or relaxed to think about blowing away their English teacher."

"Yeah, great, Leon. We'll just tell them

that 'Loose Slots' is my Indian name."

"Well, I'm just trying to help, Roger. I hate to say this, but much as I'm trying to be of assistance, the impending bankruptcy of Gammage, New York, really is your problem, not mine."

Later, her toenails painted, her spent *Allures* splayed at her feet, Serena could have sworn that, just as she completed her descent into slumber, she heard Tony say to Dick Dirigian, "You know how to make a goddamn killing these days, my friend? Get yourself declared a fucking Indian."

9
GAMMAGE, NEW YORK
JANUARY 1997

Casey Elliott and Dr. Roger Gardner agreed on one thing: The smartest man in Gammage was Dr. Roger Gardner. So it bewildered Casey to the point where he couldn't stop tugging at his ponytail when Roger revealed his newest plan for civic salvation to Casey and Barbara Menzies over coffee at the downtown Oarlucks (formerly Starbucks).

"Let me get this straight," Casey said as Barbara ferried her double cap and his grande nonfat latte to their small table. "You want us to get the entire population of the town recognized as an Indian tribe so that we can open a gambling casino?"

"I don't want you to, I'm saying it's the last best hope this town has. And," Roger said with a gesture at the silently smiling Dick Dirigian, who rounded out the foursome, "my people tell me that it's eminently 'doable,' which is a word I detest, but which fits the occasion."

Barbara wiped some cap foam off her upper lip while she wondered if Roger was being slyly condescending, whether by "the occasion" he meant a conversation with his intellectual inferiors. But her response was strictly business. "Help me understand, please, just exactly how we're supposed to justify spending taxpayers' money on what's going to sound like some kind of cockamamie get-rich-quick scheme at the same time that urgent needs in our city go unmet, would you?"

Dr. Roger Gardner's wild gray eyebrows rose in the faintest arch, while a thought flickered through his normally ad-hominem-free mind: Here's a lesbian not even Melissa Etheridge would like. But his answer, too, was strictly business. "Ms. Menzies, please help me understand exactly how you plan to justify spending taxpayers' money on plugging nearly all the holes in a terminally leaky rowboat, while anchored close by in the same harbor is a two hundred foot luxury motor yacht just begging to be of service." If Oarlucks hadn't gone over to a self-service operation at the time of the ownership change, some young kid would have come over at this point to sponge-mop the dripped contempt off the floor by

Roger's feet.

Dick Dirigian was enough of a salesman to know that this filet mignon of an idea was in dire need of the A.1. sauce of charm right about now. "Folks," he enthused, "you've been to Wowosa, right?" Casey and Barbara glumly nodded. "The place mints money. The tribe has schools that Beverly Hills would kill for, they're opening a branch of the Mayo Clinic on the reservation, their tap water now tastes better than Evian. You think a little of that magic would be bad for this community? You don't think the citizens of Gammage would lift you on their shoulders and do a war dance of gratitude for your inspired and farsighted leadership? Give me one giant gold-encrusted, diamond-studded, champagne-soaked break."

Casey stirred uneasily at this point, not because of his discomfort with the stranger's persuasiveness, but because he had just filled his diaper. The act thrilled him with private pleasure, which was the point of being a Big Baby, one of those grown-ups who suffered no incontinence but lived what they called the Diaper Lifestyle out of, so they said, choice. But something about sitting awash in his own warm, lovely urine in the leoninely intimidating presence of Dr. Roger

Gardner made Casey feel less privileged than usual, made him feel a little . . . furtive about pursuing his lifestyle at this particular moment. He struggled to get his mind back on the subject.

"Okay," Casey said finally, fixing his gaze on the black-and-white photos of the Oar-lucks coffee offerings that lined the opposite wall, "let's say we went ahead with this Indian idea, as crazy as it sounds. And let's say that we did get wet — I mean, that we did recognized as a tribe or something. Then what? I mean, Jesus, we don't know the first thing about running a casino."

"I'm sure Mr. Dirigian can address that question," Barbara Menzies shot sardonically at the visitor as she drained the last of her foam.

"You know something," he crooned brightly, "I sure as hell can."

10
WOWOSA,
CONNECTICUT
APRIL 1997

"Slots look good. Roulette . . . nice. What the hell's the matter with craps?"

Joseph Catspaw scanned the readout on the flat-panel screen that stood, with the smallest imaginable footprint, on his desk. In less time than it took for the image of Chief Rocking Bear to fill out behind the numbers, he could see that not all was well in the Craps Pavilion.

"Just a big weekend for nickel-dimers is all," Don Nightswim said, floating a trial balloon of explanation into the darkening sky of his boss's gaze. "B and Ts up from Jersey, buying discount gas on the Turnpike, packing bag lunches, from the look of our food numbers."

Joseph sat silent for a moment, a moment long enough to let Don ponder the possibility of once again paddling slingbacks and mules at Payless. Then he smiled. "It's okay, we'll just tighten up the slots for a couple of days. We'll do a *'nice.'* "

Life had gotten good for Joseph Catspaw, good enough that a slight dip in the "drop," or money flow, in the Craps Pavilion was the worst thing to happen to him all month. Running the Wowosa Casino had made him a little grayer, a little soft and cakey around the midsection, but also a very wealthy and happy man. His wife, Cheryl, who thought she had married a Brooklyn Jew trying to make a name for himself in the fashion-jeans business, now found herself living with an Indian gambling magnate who had promised her, absolutely guaranteed her, that within the year there would be a Bijan store on the reservation. The eight-year-old fraternal twins, Max and Sam, were whizzes at Hebrew, thanks to the online lessons at Yeshiva.org, and, as soon as the team of researchers from Cornell had completed the Wowosa glossary, the kids would be powering through their Indian linguistic heritage, as well.

"What else you got?" Joseph asked.

Don fiddled with his PalmPilot, then infrared an official-looking document from the Bureau of Indian Affairs onto Joseph's screen.

"The hell do they want? More comps? Tell them I'm comped out until the New Year.

The Jewish New Year." Joseph grinned as he ran his right hand along his spiky dark hair.

"Ah, it's some kind of routine advisory that they've received a new request for tribal recognition," Don said, relaxed now that the craps crisis appeared to have abated.

"Oh, yeah? Lemme see . . . the Filaquonsetts? Upstate New York? Great. More wampum to 'em." Joseph got up, his nervous Brooklyn energy impelling him to open the massive glass display case behind his desk to show Don the newest additions to his collection of souvenir figures from bad television shows. "Have you seen this? Genuine Donny and Marie dolls from the seventies."

Don didn't share his boss's peculiar passion for throwing money away on latex-and-cloth reminders of how much time he'd wasted watching TV, but he did a good job of faking it. "Man, I didn't even know they did Donny and Marie dolls."

"Only in Canada. Listen to these things." Joseph set the miniature siblings on his desk, pushed a button in the diminutive Donny's head, and in tinny doll voices the brother said, "I'm a little bit country!" and the sister replied, "I'm a little bit rock and roll!"

"That's a *cute'*, huh?" Joseph enthused.

"The Donny doll controls the timing, so she always comes in just right. Very sophisticated for the seventies."

Before Don could answer, Joseph bounded toward the door. "Jesus, I almost forgot, they're cutting revised narration tracks for the Heritage Center. Come on."

Maybe it was his background in the cutthroat fashion-jeans business, as a kid from Brooklyn getting chewed up by teams of Israeli or Lebanese brothers — companies blending the cream of Levantine mercantile skill with the ferocity of Sicilian family feuds — but Joseph Catspaw was as media-savvy as they came. He had insisted that the Wowosa complex include its own recording studio, a state-of-the-art digital facility one flight up from the mezzanine level (where platoons of part-Wowosans made big money peering down at the casino floor, alert for any signs of irregular behavior on the part of the customers or the dealers). In this studio was created the famous "War Dance Welcome," the recording that greeted each Wowosa visitor at the Casino's grand entrance with the voice of Chief Rocking Bear saying, against a background of rhythmic whoops, "How! Greetings from the people of the Wowosa Nation. Please enjoy your stay and see your change girl for any help you may need." The part of Chief Rocking Bear was played first by Casey Kasem, then, when the money started rolling into the tribal coffers, it was rerecorded by Kevin Spacey. From the studio also came the wave of radio and TV commercials that blanketed the Northeast United States with the now-unavoidable slogan "It's not wow! It's Wowosa!"

As Joseph and Don slipped into the darkened, green-felt-walled studio, the voice of James Earl Jones was already booming through the Tannoy speakers: "Testing. Testing. This is CNN. Just kidding. Sorry, Ted."

"That's fine, James," the engineer at the console said into nothing visible, since the talkback microphone was flush-mounted into the console itself. The famous actor was equally invisible, the studio behind the double-glass windows empty and unlit.

"Where is he today, Keith?" Joseph asked the engineer.

"The city."

"Asshole. For what we're paying him . . ."

"We good to go?" the unmistakable baritone asked through the ether.

"Lemme talk to him," Joseph snapped. The engineer pressed the talkback button. "James, we just want to redo a couple of speeches. The elders thought the opening wasn't — you know, respectful enough."

"The elders?" James Earl Jones sounded a tad dubious.

"Yeah. My mother-in-law, okay? We're rolling, tape costs money, let's go."

There was no tape. A computer simulation of tape was doing a computer simulation of rolling, and James launched into a reading so respectful, you could hear the somber orchestral strings behind it, though they would actually be laid in later, in Prague, where good symphony musicians worked cheap. "In 1975, there was only one surviving member of the Wowosa Nation living on tribal land. It was she who, despite the tribe's near-total-massacre by the U.S. Army in the 1840s, vowed to keep the Wowosa Spirit alive. Elder Sally Willowbark knew that spirit, the spirit of the soaring hawk, would one day again be ascendant. This . . . is that day."

Don Nightswim brandished his Palm Pilot, swung it toward Joseph, the miniaturized memo from Indian Affairs glowing on its screen. "What do we want to do about this?"

"Just a second," Joseph Catspaw warned. "We only got him for an hour. Verizon owns him for the day. James, that's great, just go

90

on and give us a nicer reading on paragraph ten."

"Nicer?" growled the voice from the Tannoys.

"Yeah. You know. Warm it up a little."

The actor cleared his throat and launched into a reading warmer than maple syrup on weekend waffles. "When news of the Casino's construction spread, the call went out across the Northeast for anyone with one-thirty-second Wowosa blood or more to Come Home. Joseph Katz, who had married a one-sixteenth Wowosa woman, did just that, bringing his business expertise to the task of running the world's largest gaming center. He changed his name to Catspaw, a historic tribal name. The rest . . . is Native American history."

"See? That's a *'nice.'* " Joseph was almost moved, despite the fact that he had written the copy himself. The power of professional delivery. "Thanks, James."

"No problem." There was the sound of a stool being moved and a heavy studio door opening and closing, then the line to the city went dead.

Joseph turned to Don Nightswim. "I gotta go to Hartford, see a guy who says he has a mint-condition Ralph Malph. You know how long it takes Indian Affairs to do anything. Put that memo in my Remember-to-Ignore file."

Don laughed. "You got it."

11
GAMMAGE, NEW YORK
JULY 1997

The Filaquonsetts had been an actual Indian tribe. Dr. Roger Gardner had found them himself, poking around in an obscure State University of New York library Web site. They were, he thought, perfect for the revival that awaited them. Pushed westward from their original location along the Massachusetts coast, they were wiped out when the remaining thirty-two members, living in poverty in upstate New York, were felled by the great influenza epidemic of the second decade of the twentieth century. They had contracted the flu from virus-infested washcloths and face towels distributed to the tribe as a charity gesture by a local Odd Fellows Lodge.

It wasn't smallpox, but it was bad enough.

The victims, before their victimhood enveloped them, were Filaquonsetts in name only. A series of massacres along the Highway of Bad Dreams had decimated the tribe's institutional memory. The oral tradition had died under the pressure of forced assimilation in communities that never cottoned to the idea of injuns in their midst. There was no record, in the SUNY database or elsewhere, of Filaquonsett ways.

"Hya hya hya. Come on, let's all do it now." Anna Manybirds was dancing around the floor of the gym at Christa McAuliffe High, her heavy crimson shawl swinging behind her as she swayed this way and that, swooping first one shoulder floorward, then the other, in the Eagle Dance. Slowly, reluctantly, some three hundred townspeople in the City of Gammage trooped down out of the stands onto the gym floor and attempted, with varying degrees of accuracy, to mimic her movements and her noises. "Hya hya hya," they murmured asynchronously. Anna was a short, thick, blackhaired woman with the broad facial features not normally associated with television anchorpeople. She was, in fact, a Tlingit, a member of a Native American tribe who inhabited southeast Alaska. The Eagle Dance was a Tlingit ritual. As far as anyone knew, it had never been performed east of British Columbia before this brittle midwinter Sunday afternoon. But making an application to be recognized as an Indian tribe required learning something about being some kind of Native American, Mayor Curtis Zorn had argued at the Selectpersons meeting where the plan was approved. "They're obviously going to send somebody here to see some Indians, so it seems to me at the very least we've got to show them some Indians."

At the persuasive urging of Dr. Roger Gardner, Dick Dirigian had agreed to be hired as a consultant on the project, for a nice little share of the eventual casino's revenue, leaving the beverage exclusivity needs of the nation's schools in someone else's hands. He confided at the meeting that he had "the best contacts for Native Americans on the planet." Then, the next morning, he called Tony Silotta's Las Vegas office in a panic, his fingers so marinated in their own perspiration, they almost slid off the telephone's keypad. "Tony, *mi amigo,* you're out West, you gotta know somebody who's got an available brave or squaw on the line," he pleaded.

"Dick," Tony said in a calm, reassuring voice, "don't get your comb-over in a tangle. I was on a celebrity cruise to Alaska last year, they had some Indians performing on the boat, doing their charming native bullshit for us. They erected a fucking totem pole during our farewell dinner. I'll make a couple of calls. Just make sure this thing holds tight on your end."

"Tony, please," Dick said, tamping down his insecurity to placate the great man, "this town is so desperate for salvation, they'd agree to be hypnotized into walking around like chickens."

"Don't be ridiculous," Tony huffed, "that's the act that closed the Dunes."

Lucy Striker was, as usual, not going along with the program. Anna Manybirds paused in her dance to share some Tlingit lore: "We have five clans in our tribe: the Eagle, the Caribou, the Elk, the Snake, and the Salmon. But you, our friends and soon to be our brothers, will be part of a new clan in our eyes: the Butterfly. Come, let's all do the Dance of the Butterfly." She began doing a set of moves and chants that, to the unpracticed eye and ear, seemed indistinguishable from the Eagle Dance. Lucy Striker stood, arms crossed, brow furrowed, between the body of townspeople Butterflying around the gym floor and the emptied grandstand. "This is just such a total waste of time and money," she mourned. Mayor

Curtis Zorn heard her as he swooped by. "She's just getting expenses," he said. Then he added, "Hya, hya, hya."

Las Vegas, Nevada, July 1997
No one had ever seen a production like *We Are Here/Nous Sommes Ici,* the latest extravaganza by Circus des Artistes. Water, flame, ice, lasers, holograms, trapezes, mimes, and clowns — it couldn't have cost any more to produce, Tony Silotta thought, if they'd dropped half the artsy-fartsy crap and thrown in a couple of hundred gold-encrusted elephants. Nevertheless, Vince and Eileen Winstanley were sitting spellbound at the front-row table they shared with Tony, Serena, and Leon Wendelkind, all of them comped by Tony's good friends at the Royal Fijian, the fabulous new Vegas hotel that actually created a lush tropical rain forest in the middle of the desert.

Tony had no business pending before the Bureau of Indian Affairs, so Leon argued to Vince that accepting the free airplane trip, standard deluxe room, all gratuities, and $100 worth of chips would not constitute an ethical problem. Vince's problem was convincing Eileen. She voiced her skepticism about taking the trip as they power-walked along the C&O Canal on a blustery afternoon.

"He's a Vegas gambling mogul, he's not inviting you out there just to show a middle-level Interior Department official a good time."

"A, we've never seen Circus des Artistes, and you've always wanted to."

"We can see them in Canada, our dollar's so strong we can buy our own front-row seats, and you won't owe anything to anybody. What's B?"

"I kind of owe Leon a favor."

"So you take him to a nice dinner. Why does this have to involve Mr. 'Those Were *Chips'?*"

She was referring to a television commercial that had briefly made Tony Silotta a familiar face to people other than the members of the Nevada Gaming Commission. In the spot, Tony bragged about the top-line entertainment he featured at his original Strip hotel, the Gold Rush, while he pretended to be tidying up one of the fabulous suites. All of sudden, Paul Anka walked into frame, looked around the suite, and asked Tony, "Have you seen that pile of chips I won last night?" Tony, playing embarrassed, turned to the camera, flashed his thousand-watt simulation of a shit-eating grin and, with a comedy take so outsized it would have shamed Shemp, said, "Those were *chips?"* The Gold Rush was imploded on live television in 1988.

"This seemed sort of important to Leon."

"Well, that should be a tip-off."

"You know, I've been around the block enough times to protect myself. If anything comes up that smells wrong, we politely excuse ourselves, pack our overnighters, and fly back to D.C. on the first available departure."

"You don't think Tony can close down the airport?"

"You're kidding."

"I am kidding. But do you?"

"No. This isn't like the bad old days of Vegas. Tony may be Italian, but that place is now more corporate than the luxury boxes at the MCI Center. Worst thing he can do is make us meet Paul Anka."

"Okay. Race you back home."

Gammage, New York

"To get the color patterns, we use different-colored reeds. Each is woven in a style that's characteristic of a particular clan. So you can always tell a basket made by an Eagle Clan member from one woven by a Caribou clan member. Yes, question."

After the dancing, Anna Manybirds had sat down on the gym floor, surrounded by a collection of Tlingit woven baskets and mats. The Gammage townspeople had joined her on the floor, although Lucy Striker had somewhat petulantly inquired why there were no folding chairs. Far more enthusiastic, Daria Long had with some time and effort hunkered her pear-shaped self down and started taking copious notes on a yellow legal pad of the various weaves and reeds introduced during the session. Toward the end of the discussion, Daria shot her hand into the air. Some of the more restless members of the audience glared at her.

"Yes, Anna, first I want to thank you for sharing so much of your culture with us today." Anna nodded a modest acknowledgment. "Even if we weren't embarking on this new adventure," Daria went on in her tremulous soprano, aching with sincerity, "just being able to make this connection with a culture thousands of years old and thousands of miles away is, to me, and I'm sure to the rest of us, is the most exciting thing to happen to this community since the national company of *Rent* came through town."

"That was filth. This is clean. So far," Arnold Lipshitz yelled out way too loud and a bit too cranky for the oceanic feeling of goodwill that Anna was trying to purvey. Arnold was not the oldest Gammage resident, but he was certainly the oldest civic activist. An octogenarian widower and retired writer (he had scrapbooks full of clippings from publications long shuttered — chatty columns from *Collier's,* once-over-lightly profiles in *Look,* think pieces from *Pageant*), Arnold took the community's survival seriously enough to be squatting on the gym floor wearing a feathered head-dress.

"You're right, Arnold, this is very clean." Daria picked up the thread of her speech, and only the loud and cranky would have suspected any condescension in her response. "But, Anna, what I'm wondering, and maybe some of the rest of us are, too, is whether there was ever any connection between your people and the people we people are linking up with, if you will."

Anna processed about half of the question before a rattle of beads announced the fact that Mayor Curtis Zorn had stood up. "Daria, I think the long and sad history of Native Americans, what with their being moved here and there around the country pretty much at the whim of the white man, suggests that there were links between and among almost all of the tribes that, unfortunately, we'll never know about. What I do know, thanks to Mr. Dirigian here" — and he nodded at Dick, who was absentmindedly picking apart one of the woven baskets — "is that Anna has done this same demonstration for the Wowosas, as well as for several other re-heritaged tribes here on the east coast, so we should be right in synch with many of their rituals."

"The Wowosas are the Clan of the Sea Bream," Anna chimed in.

Las Vegas, Nevada

"You folks are a fabulous audience," Cook E. Jarr said to the half-empty room. "You know, we're so crazy we do this again at four a.m., so stick around, drink some lightly watered booze, lose some money, and we'll see you back here in about fifteen minutes." The band slammed out a double-time, eight-bar play-off of "Lady Madonna," and for the moment, the entertainment was over.

"Last true lounge in town, my friends. Read it and weep." Tony was in an expansive, nostalgic mood, regaling Vince and Eileen and Serena and Leon with great, ribald tales of the Vegas gone by. Serena had a few of her own to share, but not in front of Tony.

"I was in here one night when Louie and Keely were cookin'," he said, assuming that everyone in the universe knew the last names of the performers, "and all of a sudden Frank walks in, Sam Butera signals the band, without skipping a beat they go right into like a jump-time rendition of 'Witchcraft,' Frank hits the stage, and they don't stop singing and screwing around and doing shtick until ten fifteen the next morning. You remember this, Reeny, all the kids from the other hotels would come over and by dawn, the fuckin' place was packed. And here's the money shot: Half the night, there's at least two chicks on the stage, servicing Frank and Louie *while they're singing.* Keely just looks on with that Indian stare, and Sam's got a woody the size of Hoover Dam, but he's got to keep leading the band!"

Vince and Eileen were experiencing a serious case of Clark County overstimulation by this point in the evening. They looked at each other for guidance as to the appropriate reaction to Tony's anecdote but, finding none, the best each could offer was a version of "Huh!" Serena sipped her old-fashioned and swayed in time to the Kool and the Gang tape blasting through the lounge, while Leon's eyes grew wide and misty. "Man, Tony, you ought to get your memory insured by Lloyd's of London," he said. "But," Leon continued, now catching the method in Silotta's madness, "speaking of Indians, Vince, I think we finally figured out how to cancel that little indebtedness of ours." Vince sat up as if a spiky metal rod had just been shoved up the length of his spinal column.

Eileen tried to mask her alarm by taking a swig of Serena's drink.

"Leon, as I said back in D.C., I really can't do anything about —"

"Tony would you excuse us?" Leon said, grabbing Vince by the elbow and steering him toward the vague demarcation point between the lounge and the casino. "Tony hates hearing people talk business in a lounge setting," he confided mid-walk. "So look, I understand that a certain long-neglected Indian tribe is seeking recognition by your agency, okay?"

Vince relaxed a little as the slots churned and chittered behind him. "A couple hundred are, Leon, which particular —"

"The Filaquonsetts. They're very special to me, okay? It's a long story."

Vince considered confiding in Leon that,

as favors went, this was a cheap one, since his boss was already leaning on him to expedite such recognitions. But a little voice just under his crew cut told Vince, "If the man wants to be grateful, let him be grateful. These people seem to take gratitude very seriously."

"I don't foresee a problem there, Leon," was all Vince said.

By the time they got back to the table, Tony was halfway through a story about Dean Martin, four hookers, and a school bus.

12
WASHINGTON, D.C.
SEPTEMBER 1997

There was a clicking sound. No doubt about it, as Assistant Secretary of the Interior Hap Matthews testified before the Subcommittee on Indian Affairs of the Senate Interior Committee, everybody who was still awake heard a clicking sound. Everybody, that is, except Hap. Having departed from his usual office uniform of gray suit and off-white shirt, accented by a battleship gray silk tie, to assume the more business-like appearance of a *dark* gray suit with a *blue* shirt and the battleship gray silk tie, Hap was concentrating on giving the Indian Affairs satrapy under him the image of a federal agency on the move, a veritable corsair of a bureaucracy, slicing through the waves of inertia and encrusted practice, leaving a wake of satisfied constituents and admiring auditors.

He had brought charts and graphs —

flowcharts, pie charts, organizational charts, bar graphs — even videotapes of tribal chiefs giving praise to the onetime instrument of their oppression. Most of the presentation had been assembled by Vince Winstanley, whom Hap had identified as a breath of fresh air shortly after Vince's arrival. Usually, Hap didn't like breaths of fresh air. They caused changes in procedure or, worse yet, policy; sometimes they even pushed for alterations of the office geography. But for Hap, who despised these congressional appearances as periodic political root canals devised by the overrated framers of the Constitution to bedevil him on a semiannual basis, Vince's work crafting a rosy-hued view of a newer, finer, nicer, fresher, cleaner, leaner, but not meaner Indian Affairs was exactly the kind of thing breaths of fresh air were supposed to do.

Indian Affairs hearings were viewed by subcommittee members as useful only for those Senators worried about the problem of excessive television exposure. No one could recall the last time even a single camera crew had taken up a position inside the chamber when this particular subcommittee met. C-SPAN, alerted to Indian Affairs hearings, opted instead to show taped sessions of the British or Canadian Parliaments.

So the only person really irritated to the point of curiosity by the clicking that accompanied Hap's presentation was the young subcommittee intern responsible for audiovisual presentations, Jennifer New Moon. A twenty-year-old, full-blooded Lakota Sioux drawn to the six-month internship by the very subject matter most members found soporific, Jennifer battled internal demons telling her that, despite the clear and focused projection of Hap's video, despite the loud and resonant quality of his voice through the subcommittee's sound system, the incessant clicking from somewhere was, somehow, her fault, and would ultimately redound to the eternal shame of her people. She began crawling under the green-cloth-covered table at which Hap spoke, checking connections with her trusty mini-Maglite, gently tugging and poking cables and adapters and male and female plugs and junction boxes and y-connectors, blowing the dust off the amplifier and peering through its ventilated cover, troubleshooting the way her dad, an appliance repairman in a small town just off the Lakota reservation, had always taught her. But, as Hap ticked off impressive signs of progress in returning tribal moneys and expediting tribal recognitions and untangling knotty sovereignty battles with state governors over taxes and highways, the clicking just persisted.

Late in his testimony, as senatorial aides began solidifying their lunch plans and even the reporter from the *Hopi News* was breathing slowly, shallowly, and noisily, Hap's administrative assistant handed him a letter. Matthews glanced at it, and the subcommittee's chairman, Senator Chuck Weems, a youngish ex-anchorman from Georgia, seized the opportunity of the pause in Hap's monologue to pose a question. "Mr. Matthews," the senator said in an accent that owed more to broadcasting than to geography, "as you know, I ascended to the chairmanship of this subcommittee thanks to being on the wrong side of a little dispute with the distinguished majority leader, but nevertheless in the seven months that I've held this position, I have tried to familiarize myself with the main issues relating to relations with our Indian friends and neighbors."

Hap could tell there would be plenty more throat-clearing before Weems got to the point, so he turned his attention to the letter. It was on Wowosa Tribe stationery, elegant Florentine paper hand-embossed with the tribe's insignia (which had, in fact, been stencil-copied off an old Navajo rug), and it was signed by Don Nightswim, the tribe's Minister of External Relations. He was responding to the request for comments on the Filaquonsett Nation's application for recognition, and his tribe had no objection at this time. A notation at the top indicated that the letter was to be sent "VIA FAX," but it had arrived in a stamped envelope three weeks after it was written. It was the only response the office had received to its request for comments.

"And so," Senator Weems was pretending to conclude, "what I'm wondering is whether there's anything we can do to speed up this process of giving these forgotten tribes the recognition they have for so long been in the process of not getting."

"Senator," Hap interrupted, "I have good news." Jennifer New Moon noticed that the clicking had stopped during the senator's mini-filibuster, but resumed the minute Hap did. "I'm in a position here today to announce that we are recognizing the Filaquonsett Tribe in upstate New York and acknowledging their petition for tribal reservation status for the area known as the

Gammage tract. I'm going to ask Mr. Winstanley, who has operational responsibility for Indian Affairs, to communicate this information to the new tribe in an appropriately timely manner."

"I hope that doesn't mean smoke signals," Senator Weems said with a chuckle. Having crawled back out from under the table, Jennifer simmered inwardly at the idea that her boss thought that comment was funny, then she was struck by a realization: As Hap pretended to laugh, moving his mouth but making no laughing sounds, the clicking sped up. She could relax. The pressure was off. The man was making the noise with his dentures.

PART TWO

13
FILAQUONSETT RESERVATION, NEW YORK FEBRUARY 1998

"We are here *live* on this historic morning, and the sounds you hear in the background are the musicians of the Gammage High School Concert Band playing the 'Filaquonsett Tribal March,' assembled from historic and ancient sources by our own Dr. Roger Gardner. Let's listen to some of this stirring and semi-native music." Earlene Hammond's voice was an odd mix of native Hoboken with the fake British accent that, along with a brief marriage to a radical genius of '60s theater, was all she had to show for two years of acting school. That voice was pouring out of radios across the Filaquonsett Reservation, a sovereign territory that had replaced, on the very latest maps, the Town of Gammage, New York.

The radio station had been reborn, thanks to a grant from the Bureau of Indian Affairs, as WQUO. The money went to buy back the license from the "Hot Jesus Talk" people, who found that the audience for Alan Keyes in the morning and reruns of Alan Keyes in the afternoon had plateaued, if a plateau can be located at the bottom of something. Now, in addition to the usual public-radio fare and the tri-annual pledge drives, the station featured a weekly exploration of the Filaquonsett Heritage, *Finding the Hawk Within,* as well as an extremely popular new five-minute afternoon news feature, *Today in Gaming.* It had originally been given the even more utilitarian title *Today in Gambling,* until Dick Dirigian e-mailed Earlene that "this usage is extremely unwise."

"Very inspiring music," Earlene observed over the second verse of what sounded like a cross between John Philip Sousa and Sitting Bull. She was squinting through her longish, rust-colored bangs in the blazing midday sun, sitting on a metal folding chair behind a card table in the Filaquonsett Casino's parking lot, which was, at this very moment, still in the process of being striped. An oilcloth painted with the station's new call letters was draped on the table's front, and that bit of display accounted for the sparse little crowd assembled around Earlene as she anchored the live broadcast of what she called "the most momentous event in Noneonta County since the library fire: the opening of the world's largest Indian casino, an event which we think will not only turn around the fortunes of our community, but which has enabled us all to reconnect with roots that, frankly, until a few months ago, I think a lot of us didn't realize we even had."

The excitement hadn't started with this momentous opening. There had been a temporary casino, slapped together by Tony Silotta within ninety days after R (for Recognition) Day, in the former Main Library (the books had been trucked to a self-storage facility two towns down the road for safekeeping. Where there had been understimulation, suddenly there was over-stimulation. Where previously had been heard only the sounds of pages turning, computer keys being quietly tapped, and occasional snoring, now the room was filled with the high-pitched drone that was the song of hundreds of new, electronic slot machines, machines that each hummed the identical frequency, a collective high-C singing of riches to pour into the tribe's newly established coffers.

Beneath the two-story-high ceiling of the

library, which was where your Homer, your Virgil, your Washington Irving used to gaze down upon the literate few, Tony had installed a ceiling of mirrored panels, reflecting the visual roar of the machines back on themselves, amplifying, multiplying the din for the eye. Fake black walls had been installed, directing one's gaze back to the action at hand, and a temporary lounge had been set up in the former children's reading area, now a place to buy drinks and hear a Rochester band named Rainy Daze perform Southern- and arena-rock classics from the '70s and early '80s. You'd have sworn it was Steve Perry of Journey standing before you, in the shiny, dark, short-sleeved shirt, dedicating a song to "Dante, who's been eating as if he's headed for the chair." But it was just Coby Fowler, who, at a time in life when most failed rockers have long since retreated to matte fabrics, had discovered the Trail of Lounges, a new circuit of entertainment venues at tribal casinos, and had re-formed the Daze, a college frat dance band that had hung on long enough to avoid success in three distinct decades.

Now, the majority of townspeople were busy trooping through the real casino, goggle-eyed — those who weren't familiar with the place from their jobs on the construction crew — at the sheer, vast, galactic size of the place. Two Wowosas and an Office Depot would fit neatly inside it. The proud tribe members were equally agog at the spectacle factor, and here the fine hand of Tony Silotta could be seen: in the massive men's and ladies' rooms, with their Tuscan-style hand-painted sinks, each bearing a different vivid floral pattern; in the sumptuous (though clashing) fabrics that carpeted the shopping arcade and canopied the entrances to the high-end stores; in the huge aquaria that lined the walls of the casino's signature restaurant, The Hungry Bear, the tanks filled with oversized tropical fish, foraging around brightly colored but non-nutritious reefs of artificial coral; and in the huge, decorated ceiling of the ground-floor's main casino, a mural painted on the bottom side of the one-way glass that recapitulated the highlights of the Sistine Chapel's ceiling, except that now all the major characters were holding, and showing, winning poker hands.

Dick Dirigian was at his most ebullient. He had blown his opening-day bonus on a $2,000 Ermenegildo Zegna blazer-and-slacks ensemble, and he reveled in his new-found dapperness as he docented crowds of locals through Club Suit, the ultra-elegant showroom Tony had built (with input from Serena, who knew a thing or two about stages), and where, all day, Gary Puckett and the Union Gap were cycling through their classic-rock hits "Young Girl" and "Woman Woman," warming the place up (in truth, running an all-day sound check) for the evening's appearance by the entertainer known in Vegas as The Indian, Wayne Newton. As Dick rhapsodized about the state-of-the-art lighting truss, the sound system that could blast you senseless as well or better than any midsummer movie, and the sight lines that cleverly afforded every audience member an excellent view of both the stage and the casino beyond, he couldn't help patting down his new hair-weave from time to time. Yes, he had sprayed it as assiduously as if he were lacing a mosquito-filled meadow with malathion, and that in itself was a new thrill, since spraying the old comb-over just left his scalp feeling sticky. But the weave was still new to Dick, and it felt good to know that, in the five minutes since he'd last oh-so-casually sent his left hand up there for a recon, nothing had moved.

Tony himself was squiring Vince Winstanley on a VIP tour of the place, showing off the "world-class dressing rooms" for the entertainers, a cash-handling facility for the casino that was "designed by the Swiss to discourage any hanky-panky," and the small facility in the rear of the casino complex where "we manufacture our own chips, to keep as many jobs inside the 'tribe' as possible."

Vince was scratching his crew cut, wondering what the BIA had wrought. "You know, Tony, since you comped Eileen and me in Vegas, it seems like I've seen more casino life than I had in my entire existence up to then."

Tony winked. "Pretty fucking good life. And as far as our Native American brethren are concerned, it kicks the shit out of squatting on your ass beside the highway hoping some tourists stop and buy one of your ratty blankets, doesn't it?"

"Yes, it does," Vince said with a certain halfheartedness, "it does kick the shit out of that."

From the catwalk where they stood, Tony waved to the foreman on the floor of the manufacturing facility. "Hey, Cal," Tony yelled, smiling broadly, "you mean those are chips?"

"Hya, hya, hya," Chief Curtis Zorn chanted into the microphone. He was close to getting a migraine from the weight of the feathered headdress that perched on his scalp, and he was close to losing his balance each time he tried to sway back and forth in what he remembered of the Eagle Dance, but he wouldn't let any of that spoil this special day. A stage was set up outside the front entrance to the casino, and the festivities were just getting under way.

"We're so proud to welcome all Filaquonsetts and their friends to this momentous day. Just eight months ago, our tribe was nothing more than a few lines in a history book. And today, look at us. Truly, on this day, the Hawk flies high."

"Hya, hya, hya," chanted the crowd.

Dr. Roger Gardner made his way to the podium. His Phi Gamma Kappa key shone in the midday sun. Phi Gamma Kappa was an honorary fraternity that existed primarily to bestow on its fortunate brethren souvenirs of membership that happened to be the spitting image of Phi Beta Kappa keys. "We prayed to Ngadala, the god of the sun and the moon, to rescue our tribe, and our valley, and our prayers have been answered," he intoned in his orotund tenor. Beads of sweat trailed from under his headdress, which looked incongruous atop Dr. Gardner's customary black three-piece suit.

"Among the beneficiaries of this fabulous new monument to the Filaquonsett Way will be our two fine schools, Blackfoot Elementary and Wounded Knee High. The sooner we get the machines rolling, the sooner our students will get their new textbooks and/or computers. So, in the name of the tribe, I hereby declare our casino . . . open!" The crowd roared its approval, all except for one dark-skinned man, wearing a single shiny braid and a dark suit. He stood at the back of the crowd, punching observations into his PalmPilot. Aside from the quiet keystrokes, Don Nightswim wasn't making a sound.

14

To: Waaaa743@aol.com
From: BabyCasey@aol.com
Cc: Babylist
Subject: Great Idea
Attachments: Caseygoogoo.jpg

I know that, privacy being the hallmark of our lifestyle, we've always chosen to have our annual conventions up to now in extremely out-of-the-way places, mainly in Canada. But the transformative experience I and my community have been through since our last DiaperCon have made me re-think that approach, not least out of the desire to stop having to experience, upon our return, the intrusive questions of U.S. Customs agents about the trunkload of enjoyed nappies. My community has recently rediscovered its ancient Indian roots and been designated the Filaquonsett Reservation. We are enjoying a major tourist boom, thanks to our state-of-the-art casino which, by the way, offers the loosest slots in the entire Northeast!

But enough self-promotion. Here's what I propose. Our former Civic Auditorium, currently being reconsecrated as the Great Meeting Place, would be the perfect site for Diapercon XII. There are meeting rooms, a wonderful main hall, and, best of all for our needs, seating is on concrete benches, so our insurance premiums for rental of the facility would be much, much lower than usual. Plus, for the hours after our meetings and seminars and such, there's all-night gaming!

I realize that what I'm suggesting involves bringing a much higher profile to our lifestyle. Maybe it's time. Maybe, you should pardon the expression, we've grown up enough to be able to stand unashamed before the world, or at least a small tribal community in the upper Northeast, and say, "We are Big Babies. Hear us . . . ," and then whatever we want to say to complete that thought.

Let me know your reaction. Oceans of love,

BabyCasey

15
FILAQUONSETT RESERVATION, NEW YORK
APRIL 1998

"Ladies and Gentlemen, I haven't seen such commotion in the meeting room of the Council of Elders since the group was the old Board of Selectpersons. Chief Curtis Zorn is banging the buffalo head on the dais to try to restore some semblance of order, but I think, judging by the results, he's going to have to switch to an older buffalo." Earlene Hammond was back at her traditional seat, anchoring coverage of the council meetings for WQUO. She was elated to be once again the media queen of Noneonta County. During "the troubles," as she had taken to describing the period of her exile, she had moved to Syracuse and organized performances in her spacious rented living room by obscure and eccentric singers and poets. It had earned her a modicum of money (you could charge fifty to seventy-five dollars for rare local appearances by Dave Frishberg or Nikki Giovanni), and a series of noise and traffic citations by the local zoning board. All things being equal, it was good to be back.

"And now, May — excuse me — Chief Zorn seems to have restored order, so let's go back to his microphone."

"I'd like to once again recognize Elder Menzies."

"Look, I recognize that there are a number of needs in this community that casino revenues can help meet, and nobody's more in favor of that than I am," Barbara Menzies said to a chorus of boos. "But let's just think for a minute about what the Native American Hall of Fame can mean to all of us. It will put this community even more on the map than we already are. Maybe even, you know, on a much bigger map. But it's also going to serve to consolidate our claim to being a real Indian community, and not just a money-grubbing operation like Wowosa. In other words, I guess what I'm saying is, before we all start fighting over the golden eggs, we should be doing something . . . to help save some eggs for the goose that's laying them." Menzies punctuated her conclusion by swinging her microphone sharply away from her, which cued another angry eruption from the audience.

"It looks like we may be here straight

through the night," Earlene told her listeners, "so let me take just this one minute, while they're talking about money, to suggest that you are the U in public radio."

When order was restored in the hearing room, Kingsley Partridge, a thin, distinguished, graying, boating-every-Saturday-till-it-snows representative of the Smithsonian took to the podium. The Smithsonian had just dedicated an Indian museum in the last piece of buildable space on the National Mall, and Partridge had taken two trains and one bus to come here tonight, to explain why a Native American Hall of Fame that could, with its lava flow of casino money, buy every indigenous bone in the country, every blanket, every arrowhead, every last stray eagle feather, would inevitably hurt his Indian Museum, which had to do battle for congressional funds with other worthy causes, like new bombers and aircraft carriers not desired by their respective armed services. But Barbara Menzies wasn't paying very close attention to Partridge's elegant appeal. Sitting back in her Elder chair, she was doing homework. Specifically, she was reviewing some of the fine points of dealing blackjack.

The real growth industry in town these days was dealer schools. Three had opened up since R Day, and two more were awaiting their final permits. Dr. Roger Gardner, calling upon his reputation for, if not quality in education, at least persistence at it, won the first license for the Angry Elk Academy of Casino Arts. It wasn't all luck. He had suggested in a closed session of the Council of Elders, convened to discuss the purchase of new carpeting for the Council chamber, that there should be licensing for dealer schools — to protect the tribespeople from an "element" that so frequently preys on honest gaming ventures. The unspoken suggestion to the Elders, that licensing of schools could keep Scorsese-type people from taking over their good thing, was enough to win a unanimous vote. Before the decision was posted on the Council of Elders's Web site, Dr. Gardner was first in line with his application. Timing is everything.

All Barbara Menzies had known about the queen of hearts up to now was that it was the name of a lesbian bar in Toronto. But as soon as the ink was dry on the R Day proclamation, she quit her paying job as bookkeeper for the Oarlucks coffee store. "I can make more money in a night as a blackjack dealer," she told Casey Elliott after a council meeting, "than I can in a

129

week at Oarlucks." Casey fingered his gray-ing ponytail thoughtfully, a warm feeling suffusing him that, for once, emanated from thoughts of wealth. Then he quickly recon-nected with his Greenness, asking sheep-ishly, "They'll still have the fairtrade coffee, though, won't they?"

Soon, Barbara was becoming adept at the secrets of the shoe, at recognizing card counters before they hurt the evening's drop, at the hand movements that subtly signaled trouble at the table to the ever-vigilant eyes upstairs. Her instructor was Billy October, who had dealt blackjack on the *Pirate's Chest* gambling boat moored just outside Shreveport for two years. His career on the vessel had been cut short when his motion sickness flared up, scaring potential players away from the table where, word of mouth had it, "the guy throws up on the cards."

There were seventeen people in Barbara's class, including Ed Claypool, an affable, gray-haired gent who had taken early retire-ment after two decades of teaching social studies at McAuliffe, and, oddly enough, Lucy Striker. Barbara was dying to ask Lucy, whose wardrobe consisted of the cheaper end of the softer side of Sears, where she got the thousand-dollar tuition fee for the Academy, but Billy kept the classes fast-moving and demanding. Unlike players, who were adrift in a sea of choices at the blackjack table, dealers were bound by a rigid set of rules. That's what Barbara was going over in her head as the debate about the Native American Hall of Fame swirled through the Elders' chamber: What to do on a soft 17.

Billy didn't promise his students a job if they graduated, but nobody in the class thought it was unusual that one of the Tribal Elders, a certain Ms. Menzies (one of the few who still insisted on the Ms.), got a plum swing shift assignment even before her diploma slithered out of the giant Xerox machine at Kinko's. The lack of subtlety in the casino's decor was echoed in its approach to local worthies. On opening day, the secretary of the police chief, playing a $5 slot machine, won a jackpot. The payoff: a Mercedes-Benz convertible. When Dick Dirigian asked him about the wisdom of possibly choreographing such a far-fetched stroke of luck, Tony Silotta smiled, showing perhaps forty-eight snow-white jewels of dentition. "The police chief himself winning — that would be unwise. This was just kind of goofy."

16
FILAQUONSETT
RESERVATION
AUGUST 1997

"And what's your name, sweetheart?" Wayne Newton inquired.

"Serena."

"Can I tell you something? That's a beautiful name."

"Thanks. Did you like the facilities?"

"Beautiful place, but I expect nothing less of Mr. Silotta. He's a first-class type of guy all the way. You know, I tell all the people I work for to pay me in gold bars, but Tony's operation is one of the few that follows through on that." Wayne's eyes narrowed in curiosity. "Didn't you used to be a dancer at the Trop?"

"I was a covered dancer, yeah, but never at the Trop. That place always gave me the willies."

"Yeah," Wayne said, putting his left hand on Serena's right knee. They were sitting in the VIP lounge after The Indian's opening-night show. Sweat still glistened on his brow.

"I know what you me —"

Wayne had never seen a curtain come down as fast as this one did, a big black curtain, with a starburst design radiating out from its center, a spreading blackness that made it clear that, as far as consciousness was concerned, tonight's show was over.

"I know the Native American Hall of Fame is a great idea, Mr. Mayor, but, in truth, it's simply not enough." Daria Long was standing over her Viking range, cooking Wiener schnitzel for Curtis Zorn.

"Call me Chief," Curtis said modestly. "Obviously, as revenues start to stream in, there'll be plenty of resources for whatever we think we need, so —"

Daria, pear-shaped in her mid-forties but now evolving toward her melon-shaped fifties, with a mop of short, steel-gray Brillo atop her head, rattled the Calphalon ten-inch sauté pan so hard, the veal cutlets pirouetted in their butter bath. "Look, Curtis, it's just not good enough. You know we're not Indians. I know we're not Indians. We really have to do something to give back to the people on whose backs we're riding to this great prosperity we're expecting."

Seated at Daria's kitchen table, Curtis

munched thoughtfully on a carrot stick. What was her problem now? He knew what her personal problem was. She'd been married for twenty years to her college sweetheart. Together, they'd become momentarily famous for organizing the nation's largest "Death to Disco" demonstration at the University of Wisconsin, Madison. They had a model marriage, raised two model children, and then savaged each other in a model divorce. After making her life a living hell for two years, her ex-husband opened a law practice in Poughkeepsie specializing in conflict resolution. Daria threw herself into civic activism, centering on the arts. She lobbied the Selectpersons to create an Arts Commission, she hectored them to make her its first chairperson, she intimidated local businesses into submitting to a 1 percent for Art tax. She also invited over for one of her grandly Teutonic dinners every remotely eligible man in the county. Tonight it was Curtis's turn.

The cutlets arrived on the table at the same time as Daria's Big Idea. "Let's commission a series of public art pieces on Indian themes and create a Native American Sculpture Park — a NASP."

Breading and veal filled Curtis's mouth, muffling the question, "What's a NASP?"

"I just told you. A Native American Sculpture Park. Want some noodles?" Curtis thought to himself that Daria must be one of the ten people left in the country who called that dish "noodles" instead of "pasta." "Sure, I'll have a lit—" Before he could finish the word, a pound of thick, buttered noodles plopped on his plate like a fat lady on a bus bench in August.

Now Curtis's comment was muffled almost to the point of incomprehensibility by a mouthful of semolina. "Where could we put this . . . this NASP?"

"I was thinking of the wildlife refuge. It's the only open space in the vicinity that hasn't been commandeered for casino parking, and it's public land, so . . ."

"So, but isn't it supposed to be a refuge for wildlife? I mean, isn't that how it got the name? How does a collection of sculptures fit into that? Mmm, these noodles are really beautifully buttered."

"It's simple, my darling. Native Americans revere wildlife. The sculptures pay tribute to Native Americans. So the park enhances our appreciation for both wildlife and Indians, and it gives us a stature in the arts world that a casino by itself can never hope to afford."

"Even with the mural on the ceiling?"

Daria lowered her voice to her darkest baritone. "Let's not even talk about Mr. Silotta's taste in art, please." Then, turning back to the kitchen, she sang in a cheery soprano, "Save some room for the strudel."

The next morning, Curtis was jogging down to his office at tribal headquarters, in the old Manufacturers Hanover building, when his cell phone rang. In one of the first of what he regarded as his new entitlement of discretionary purchases, Curtis had sought out a retro cell phone model on which one of the ringtone options was a digital simulation of the ringing of an old-fashioned analog phone. "This is the Chief," he said, mainly because he still couldn't get used to the sound of "Chief Zorn." Something about that phrase clanked in his ears.

"Mayor — or Chief, I guess it would be — Mike Schwarzwelder here, from Wal-Mart Corporate, we had a chat a little while back."

"I vaguely remember," Curtis said, though every millisecond of his humiliation during that conversation was long since imprinted on his cortex.

"Just wanted you to know, in case you were wondering, we're in the middle of this annual review we do of all the locations we've rejected for stores in the past five years, we run the numbers from scratch, and see what's changed, and, goodness gracious, your town, or reservation, whatever it is you folks choose to call it, it's scoring very, very highly indeed on our little program here."

"Isn't that something," Curtis mused, just before doing a credible digital simulation of hanging up.

17
Wowosa,
Connecticut
September 1998

"Aw, Jesus, not again." The dulcet Brooklyn tones of Joseph Catspaw ricocheted through the cathedral-ceilinged living room of the two-hundred-year-old house he had bought and let his wife lovingly restore on the south end of the Wowosa Reservation. He and Cheryl were just returning from a VIP trip ("with the Kinder," as he loved to say) to Disney World, and they were greeted upon their return with a telltale pool of water on the new oak flooring, right beneath the spot where the new second story joined the original one. Little areas of plaster had turned to blistered cottage cheese over their heads, and now a drop of house-filtered rainwater landed on Joseph's spiky shiny black hair and lazily, almost contemptuously sauntered down his forehead. "Son of a bitch. Goddamn son of a bitch," he said. Then he added, "Kids, go up to bed."

As Max and Sam reluctantly trudged up

the stairs, clutching their personally auto-graphed Michael Eisner action figures, Cheryl faced her husband accusingly. "I told you not to use an Arab contractor, didn't I? Didn't I? Don't even try to deny it. But, no, you had to be mister open-minded, mister tolerant, you had to be mister liberal and fair, so, fine. So here we are, for the third time in two years, having to call up that creep and listen to him yell at us like *we're* the ones who can't speak English." "First of all, as I've said maybe a million and a half times, Shabshub is not an Arab, he's Leba-nese, there's a big difference."

"They all talk like they're gargling, that's all I know."

"Fine. *I'll* call him," Joseph sighed.

"No, no, that's okay;" Cheryl said while bringing a five-quart Le Creuset pot in from the kitchen, "I'm sure he's changed his at-titude toward women by now." She placed the pot beneath the leak, then hustled off to get towels to sop up the pool. "Just, next time you want to show how tolerant you are;" she yelled from the kitchen, "go give some money to the Red Crescent or some-thing, but in the future can we please stick to contractors who didn't get their licenses at a bazaar?"

■ ■ ■ ■

A couple of hours later, in the VIP bar at Wowosa, the Thirsty Caribou, Joseph was sharing some man talk — that is, complaining about women — with Don Nightswim over champagne and pretzels. He felt safe confiding in Don because his aide was being polygraphed once a week. It was Joseph's little adjustment when he learned, shortly after hiring Don Nightswim, of the man's interesting propensity for creating alternate lives for himself. Don's first wife, for example, had no idea that he had taken a second wife in Mahwah, New Jersey, four months into their marriage. Don's talent and compulsion were so evenly matched that he had managed to live two separate lives, with two separate families, selling shoes at two separate Paylesses, for three years. Shedding his African American identity for a Native American one, trading multiple braids for one, was child's play for such a man.

"I didn't used to take this crap from Cheryl, you know," Joseph hissed.

"No, I know, man. I mean, I didn't know you back then, but —"

"She was just this really pretty Catholic girl straight out of a community college on

Long fucking Island, you know what I mean, just on the prowl for a guy to marry and get her pregnant."

"I know the type," Don said, nursing his bubbly while Joseph poured himself another fluteful. "My first wife was like —"

But Joseph was in no mood to listen to somebody else's life story. "So, you know, in my own mind, I was really big shit, I mean, I was gonna cover the world's female asses with my very own brand of denim, right? She was just this sexy little shiksa who was getting off at the thought of being at my side, bearing my children, and, oh, by the way, having signing privileges on my Platinum Card."

"Well, you know, that's just a certain type of —"

"So everything is going smoother than shit through a goose, until the day she figures out that I'd, you know, done a major-league *'cute'*."

One of the main compensations for the great, towering assholes you had to deal with in the women's jeans business was the fact that you were also never far from a lavish buffet of attractive and semi-attractive young (and, to be honest, semi-young) women — models, assistants, photographers' aides, wholesalers' secretaries, de-

141

partment store buyers, fashion editors, magazine space sellers, advertising copywriters, freelance fashion "journalists" — and this was a buffet at which Joseph Catspaw believed in going back for more. He was a horndog, a satyr, a charming and insatiable schmoozer, and an ambitious sexual athlete.

Joseph had used tales of his continued adventures on the wild side to curry the friendship, if not the admiration, of the men he worked with. Don, whose own experience with women was, like his experience with powerful men, one of gaining their favor with his good looks and smarts and losing it soon after with his strange gift for alternative realities, was among the admirers.

"It was six years ago last August," Joseph said through a mouthful of pretzels. "I had been taking a few too many weekend business trips up to Saratoga because my executive assistant at the jeans company was this Eurasian girl named Coral."

"And you were her reef?"

"I was her — will you let me tell the story, please? Jesus. But so far, Cheryl's none the wiser. So this particular Sunday night, I'm a little schnockered, I'm a little tired, you know, like who wouldn't be? I'm driving the Jeep back down the Sawmill Parkway, I'm kinda weaving but I get home okay, everything's nice, the kids are asleep, Cheryl's watching AMC, I figure, case closed. Now it's Monday morning, Cheryl goes out to the garage looking for some old *House & Garden* magazines or some shit like that, and she just happens to glance over at the Jeep, and she notices there's this dent in the hood. She comes back in the house just as I'm heading out to get my nuts cut off by the two brothers from Haifa, and she says, very sweetly, 'Joe, honey, that's a pretty big dent in the Jeep's hood. It almost looks like it was made by a human body banging into the hood over and over again.' "

"Hello," Don singsonged.

"Long story medium-short, ever since then, she's got my schlong on a choke chain. You know, 'cause I do love the kids and she really was ready to walk. So, I've done a *'nice,'* and she's been on redder alert than the NSA on DefCon 7. So yeah, enough about my problems, what's up?"

"Well, you told me not to bother you about that new casino until it affected our drop."

"Yeah, let them find out how hard it is to do this job right. For Christ's sake, they're a bunch of goddamn am—"

Don took a chance and interrupted. "While you were enjoying family obligations with Goofy, we went down two-tenths of a percent. And they're not amateurs. Even though the names on the licenses are those of some Filawhatsits, it turns out the brains behind the place is Tony Silotta."

"Fuckin' Mother of Christ. I leave for five minutes to check out some *Charlie's Angels* dolls and do something age-appropriate for my kids, and you let the world's largest freestanding casino go straight down the fucking toilet. Unbelievable. What kind of an idiot are you? What the fuck you trying to do to me? You sure Silotta's involved?"

Don decided to answer only the last question. "I've checked it out eight ways to Friday. They've had some rocky moments with the new dealers, but he's straightened it out faster than a . . . I don't know, faster than a . . ."

Before Don Nightswim could finish his simile, Joseph was sprinting straight through the Golden Mile O' Slots, and hammering the up button for the private elevator like it was the nurse's call button in the ICU. Finally, in his office, he got his anger off the boil by spending some quality time with little Donny and Marie, until he started discerning the outlines of a plan. It was a little bit country, and a little bit rock and roll.

18
FILAQUONSETT RESERVATION, NEW YORK DECEMBER 1998

"Silver Bells, silver bells, it's Christmas time at Filaquonsett . . ." The customized carol, part of a package of special versions of Christmas classics performed by Johnny Elegant, the number-one Barry Manilow impressionist in all of Las Vegas, echoed through the casino complex, its gentle waltziness playing counterpoint to the increasingly frantic search of Elder Barbara Menzies for Just the Right Gift. Two months earlier, a tiny, fortyish, African-American woman had sat down at Menzies's blackjack table. She was, Barbara thought at the time, smaller than most twelve-year-olds, five feet at most, but with flashing brown eyes, a crooked smile, and a wicked wit, all of which she displayed while she kept her two-hundred-dollar stake from disappearing entirely over the course of two hours. Menzies was hit with a smitten stick, and when the woman left her table, the Elder took a chance and asked for her e-mail address.

Now, Barbara Menzies was barreling through Le Q, the marble-lined shopping arcade that stood across Wisdom of the Ancestors Boulevard from the casino, a matching money magnet. Serena Silotta, asked by Tony to help design the arcade, had simply named her twenty favorite stores on Madison Avenue and gone back to sleep. So here Barbara was on her afternoon break, trying to find the perfect gift for this diminutive, exotic woman who produced rock shows in Boston. Escada? Etro? Tourneau? Elder Menzies didn't want to pull tribal rank, she had twenty minutes before she had to punch back in, and she pinballed back and forth across the marbled hallways, certain in the knowledge that, correctly calibrated, this purchase would be the key to her new dream: a black Christmas.

"It's fucking freezing out here, Dick."

"We're standing on ice, Chief. It's supposed to be freezing."

"I know, but —"

Earlene Hammond's frantic hand signals from beyond the edge of the ice finally succeeded in alerting Chief Zorn and Dick Dirigian to the fact that they were standing at a live microphone, audible throughout the just-opened Caribou Arena, redolent with the aromas of fresh paint and new carpeting and tapas bars scattered around the mezzanine level, and on the air. "We apologize for a momentary delay in the resumption of normal tasteful programming," she blurted to her listenership.

"Christ," Dick Dirigian whispered to the chief, "if we're so freaking live, let's get on with it."

"I'm there," Zorn whispered back, then turned to the mic and the crowd beyond. "Ladies and gentlemen, we Filaquonsetts don't necessarily have Santa Claus or Christmas as part of our tribal tradition . . ." At this point, some scattered booing broke out in the cheap seats (although, in fact, admission was free on this ceremonial occasion). The chief, his fingers yellowing and numbing, pressed onward.

"But it sure looks like Santa, or the Great Elk, or whoever, has been very good to us this year, and here's tribal consultant Dick Stillwater to share the exciting news with us."

To a smattering of sounds that he chose to interpret as applause, the newly re-monikered Dick Stillwater slid past Chief Zorn. "Ladeeees and gentlemen," he said, basking in the reverberations of his voice ricocheting around the glass-walled luxury boxes that lined the top level of the arena, "please welcome . . . the banner . . . bearing the insignia of the newest National Hockey League expansion franchise: *your Filaquonsett Scalpers!*"

The PA system exploded with the loudest tribal drumming ever heard on Planet Earth. Now there were real cheers from the crowd, clapping and hooting not so much for the presentation of a banner, but for the expectation of big-league hockey that, just steps away from the rink, you could bet on in legal, climate-controlled comfort. Dick Stillwater, who had brokered the precedent-shattering deal with the league — like other pro sports, a bit shy of the association with gambling until Dick's unguent of suasion penetrated the corporate skin — tried to scratch a spot right under his feathered headdress, but the popping flashbulbs made him think better of that idea. Instead, he leaned over to Chief Zorn, putting his hand protectively over the microphone, and whispered, "If this doesn't give Wowosa a terminal case of pecker-shrinking franchise-envy, I don't know what will."

"These are diaper boosters. Have you ever done the diaper modification where you take Attends and the Overnight Promise pads and —"

"And a glue gun? Been there, thanks. If I wanted to spend that much time on a construction project, I'd work on my house."

"Well, that's exactly how we felt. See, these come ready-made, and . . ."

Casey Elliott was strolling through Hall A of the Chatting Eagle Conference Center, hearing snatches of conversation from the more than one hundred exhibitors and the nearly two thousand attendees, so to speak, at what he already knew to be the biggest DiaperCon ever. Toddler Productions had taken over the conference center and several hundred rooms at the Westin, and so far, nothing but happy babies, as far as the eye could see.

Casey wandered over to the casino, being buffeted by crowds as soon as he entered, crowds flocking to the slots. Theme slots were all the rage, and celebrity- and movie-themed slots were the hottest. Filaquonsett had bought the top of the line: the *Titanic* slots, where the animated ship shuddered every time you lost; the Sir Paul McCartney slots, which played Wings classics through-out the slot-playing experience (Yoko Ono and Michael Jackson had blocked use of The Other Catalog), and the Howard Stern slots, where, every time you pulled the lever, Howard spanked a stripper. The building itself, designed by Oliver Ney, the Robert Trent Jones of the casino-design world, was a trapezoid. The idea, as Ney had explained it in a glossy, four-color, thirty-six-page proposal, was to ensure that subsequent interior design plans would minimize the use of ninety degree angles. Casinos had learned to shun right angles, like clocks, as part of the normal world of limits and common sense that patrons were escaping. So there was a circular bar, its countertop inset with poker machines; there were walls and partitions meeting at oblique and acute angles. There were curvilinear panels and dividers alive with carvings and hangings and paintings depicting trees and animals that Dr. Gardner's extensive Google search indicated were important to Native American traditions. A stained-glass rendition of two otters frolicking separated the high-roller card tables from the nickel-dimers, and a twelve-foot-high carving of dam-building beavers loomed over the area where, on one side, actual dealers worked actual blackjack tables and, on the other, machines appealing to the more fearful gambler featured a virtual dealer, the same mid-twentyish, pug-nosed blond's face replicated on the screens of a dozen identical machines. She was filmed looking to both sides of the machine and calling out the start of a game, then, on a second screen beneath her, electronic cards were dealt to player and dealer. At game's end, the same look back and forth, and then the dealing started again.

As Casey turned to his right, what looked like a translucent curtain — except that it was a solid piece of opaque gold-flecked Plexiglas — inlaid with gilded fish glinting in alpine sunlight marked the entrance to an area with yet another innovation, the virtual roulette wheels, presided over by "dealertrons," handsome young men and slightly Asian-looking women, all depicted in the motion-capture animation style so popular with video gamers. "Thirty-three black," one barked metallically at Casey, although he noticed that the lips weren't really forming those words.

Just past the three-story granite-and-stone waterfall, Casey made his way into one of the three gift stores that lined the periphery of the casino building — income-producing amenities that served the additional purpose of further disorienting visitors. In Gift Store Alpha, he marveled at the range of the tribe's own retail offerings: soaps and candles made by actual Havasupais, pine-bark plaques offering sentences of Hopi wisdom that could motivate the businessperson, CDs and DVDs of soft-rockin' Choctaws, the Broken Arrow Leather Collection for Men and Women, and then, just before you got to the soft drinks and buffalo jerky, a selection of evening gowns for the women whose husbands had announced upon arrival that they had reservations for the dinner show (dress code strictly enforced). He bought a liter of Native Water ("As Pure as the Day the White Man Arrived"), and started back toward the conference center, when, just past the showroom box office, Elder Barbara Menzies almost plowed into him head-on, the collision broken only by a large Coach shopping bag.

"Late for a big *deal?*" Casey quipped with what he thought was almost Gardnerian wit.

"Merry Christmas," she grunted, resuming the trot toward her table.

Crossing the circular VIP driveway, Casey paused to stare back in admiration at the casino building and almost backed into Earlene Hammond, fresh from the arena and beaming in spite of the looming physical contact with her least favorite Elder. "Darling, I was just heading into the Craps Pavilion to celebrate the good news."

"Sorry, I've been in . . . in a conference. What's the news?"

"We got Garrison! We outbid goddamn Buffalo!"

Casey, so Green that he had actually proposed that the casino have a solar-powered marquee, thought, but Jim Garrison's been dead for years. Fortunately, he didn't articulate the observation.

In fact, Dr. Roger Gardner had taken some of the tribal largesse and transformed the auditorium of Wounded Knee High School into a fiber-optic-wired, fully lit, ready-for-prime-time, broadcast-capable facility that seated 2,200, and this year the *Prairie Home Companion* people had accepted Earlene's offer and opted for that space over their usual visit to Buffalo's Masonic Hall. The generous location bonus had helped, as had the assurance of very loose slots discreetly placed in the star's dressing room. Letting Earlene move on to try to double November's pledge-drive proceeds, Casey had another thought: I hope one day I love someone as much as she loves that radio station.

Within ten minutes, Casey was back where he wanted to be, in Meeting Room Owl, for an afternoon seminar on "Fasteners: What the Next Century Holds."

19
WASHINGTON, D.C.
FEBRUARY 1999

There was a new Senate in session now, a couple of key seats out West had changed hands in the election, and the pressure from the Indian Affairs Subcommittee of the Senate Committee on the Interior was off Hap Matthews. Hap, in turn, had eased off on Vince Winstanley. So, though the court-ordered repayment of mineral royalties was still inching its way through the bureaucracy and the courts, the speed-up of Indian tribe recognition had been given a lower priority. The increase in attention had been de-increased. The acceleration had been de-accelerated.

Also, the importance of Vince's job to the Winstanley family had been given a new, lower emphasis. His wife, Eileen, had been discovered by Tony Silotta, whose appetite for decorative, or at least noticeable, art vastly exceeded that of the universities and businesses for whom she had been consulting. During the ground-breaking ceremonies for the temporary casino, Tony had struck up a conversation with Eileen. Before Chief Zorn had lifted the ceremonial spade and called upon the assistance of the Almighty Falcon, Tony had offered her a job with The Silotta Organization, at a salary level where she was out-earning her husband by a factor of three, and with a budget that enabled her to seek out interesting objects, fabrics, and furnishings wherever the muse and a first-class ticket might lead her.

Eileen was flustered and flattered. Recalling her suspicion of Mr. "Those Were Chips?" she was a little embarrassed that he now seemed to find her so indispensable. So she was almost reluctant to share the news with Vince that night when, back from a day meeting with Filaquonsett tribal officials, he met her for dinner in the Motel 6 vending machine room. But her hesitation was short-lived. Vince had always been more attracted to security than to money, and he was delighted to learn that he could dial down the financial motivation even more. He had celebrated by buying his wife a box of New York State chardonnay from the "Adult Beverages" machine.

So now, enjoying the new low-pressure

environment where he was expected to do nothing more than keep Indian Affairs out of the news, Vince Winstanley was sitting in his office in the Reagan Building, considering whether, in the middle of his fifth decade, it was finally time to grow out his crew cut, when a visitor entered. This in itself was unusual. Vince, like so many folks in his profession, did most of his business without face-to-face contact. He operated through letters, memos, e-mails, phone calls, faxes, conference calls, video conferencing — every available form of mediated communication. This impersonal mode was especially common at Indian Affairs, where, until quite recently, most of the agency's clients could barely afford to send a postcard to Washington, let alone travel there.

Also, this visitor was unannounced. Vince scanned his desktop computer's calendar program to see what was scheduled for the current hour; it contained only the acronym PLN, which was Vince's assistant Karmen's little joke: the initials stood for "post-lunch nap." In these becalmed days, Vince was often found in the head-on-desk position when Karmen came in from the three o'clock Starbucks run. The visitor nodded, took a seat on the office couch, and placed a gold-colored metallic briefcase down on the standard-issue coffee table in front of him. The case made a loud, almost threatening *thwank* on the table. Eyeing his visitor, Vince came to the intuitive conclusion that the sound was intended to be more than almost threatening.

"The Filaquonsett casino," the dark-haired, stockily built stranger said in a guttural grunt, "it needs to be de-approved." Vince's head instantly swam with inappropriate thoughts: How could an inanimate object like a casino "need" anything? How could such an un-Washington type of fellow use a Beltway jargon classic like "de-approved?" What was in the metallic case? The stranger emitted two quick clucking sounds from the right side of his mouth, winked his left eye confidingly, and abruptly rose, dragging his case along the table to, Vince thought, emphasize the weight of whatever was inside it. Then he reached into his double-breasted Italian suit — the $399 Men's Wearhouse kind — fished out a business card, and flipped it onto Vince's table. He turned to say one more thing: "I can find my own way out."

After the door slammed, Vince Winstanley took off his suit jacket to allow his drowning armpits to come up for air. Then he noticed two things: the man's gold-colored case had left deep scratch marks in his table, and the business card was blank.

20
FILAQUONSETT
RESERVATION
MARCH 1999

"There is one thing we believe above all others," Dick Stillwater intoned solemnly, "and that is to treat all of our players in the Filaquonsett Way." He smiled, crinkling his tan, and nodded his head humbly as if seeking the approval of the tribe's many gods.

"What does that mean exactly?" asked Mike Bliss, the prematurely bald young interviewer from *Weekly Gaming News*, the bible of the gambling and casino industries.

"Ah" — Dick Stillwater sighed, fingering his ceremonial headdress and sipping a mixture of herbal tea and Jack Daniels — "it is a way of peace, of reconciliation of opposites, of receptivity to harmonic vibrations, of happy submission to natural cycles."

"So, reconciliation of opposites — you don't mean there are no winners and losers in your gaming operations?" Bliss asked dubiously.

"Natural cycles," Dick responded with a weariness borne of having to teach the white man so many obvious things. "There are winning cycles and losing cycles. Our visitors are always welcome back to experience yet another of nature's cycles. Care for a Triscuit?"

Later, as Bliss was shooting some head shots of Dick for the article ("We didn't have to take our own photos until the paper got bought," he explained apologetically), Dick got an "urgent" message on his pager. With a hurried apology of his own, he threw off his headdress and sprinted out his office door, leaving the reporter to pry one last snack treat from the bowl that now sat under the feathers.

Anna Manybirds looked scared and bewildered. "Hya, hya," she said breathlessly as Dick Stillwater trotted into the third-floor ballroom of the Filaquonsett Casino.

"Drop the redskin crap, what's wrong?" Dick said, a coat or two of his usual smoothness having rubbed off in the rush.

"I was just teaching my five o'clock class in chanting . . . we were doing the Hopi farewell to the setting sun, which as you know is a very slow and thoughtful chant" — Anna's normally placid manner was returning at the mere thought of the Hopi chant, while Dick was starting to sweat noticeably from under his hair weave as she continued to beat around the goddamn bush — "and all of a sudden, this came through that window." She placed in Dick's hands a large paving stone, painted with an intricate, ominous, red-and-black Native American design. "That's the Wowosa pictogram for danger," she whispered timorously, not wanting to panic the few townspeople still awaiting the resumption of class.

"This is the only section of the casino that has windows," Dick said pensively, more to himself than to Anna. He was trying on a mode of being he had long aspired to, but had only rehearsed in his dreams — the suave detective coolly assessing the few clues before him. In his dreams, though, he didn't sweat.

"I guess," Anna said, her anxiety level rising again. "Is something wrong?"

"I believe the Filaquonsett Way is to see all of life as a series of Nature's cycles," Dick said. Anna nodded, for this was indeed part of the CD-ROM of that title on which she and Dr. Roger Gardner had collaborated. "Well," Dick added, stashing the suspicious paving stone under his jacket, "we may be entering the Shit Cycle."

21
IRVINGTON, NEW YORK APRIL 1999

Lucy Striker had moved. The rent on the small stone cottage she'd occupied since she was young and plain had tripled, then quadrupled. Not even the income she was enjoying as one of the tribe's dealers on the 6 a.m. to 2 p.m. shift, the one assigned to the professionally adequate but glamour-challenged, could equip her to deal with the new Filaquonsett economy. So she'd packed up her boxes of newspaper clippings, her manila folders full of city department reports and commission findings, as well as her clothes, her thirteen-inch, black-and-white, no-brand TV, her three cats and their beds and boxes, and her practice blackjack shoe, and she U-hauled it all down State Route 28 to Irvington, the next incorporated community to the south. There, she found a second-floor apartment in an eighteenth-century brick fortress, and, in the hours when she wasn't dealing or commuting up to tribal territory, she began attending meetings of the Irvington Town Council and studying up on what ailed this little community.

The chief problem in Irvington right now was the Filaquonsett casino. Town Sheriff Randy (Pete) Vinson put it bluntly at a Council meeting, right after Lucy had been told that she'd exceeded her allotted time for public comment, and would she please, *please* sit back down. Vinson, a tall, over-tanned, bulky man in a beige uniform, minced no words, possibly because these meetings were not being broadcast: "A big part of our budget comes from speeding tickets. I don't want to say that we can compete in that department with some of the communities in the Deep South who pioneered this particular revenue stream, but, as the members of this Council should know, we do pretty frigging well. Pardon me, ladies. Now, I invite you folks to go out to State Route 28 and see what's been going on out there. With the increase in traffic incidenting through our community with the sole purpose of responding on up to the casino, the average speed on that road has just dropped like a stone, to the point of which where, the only way any of my men could write a speeding ticket anymore is if we down-corrected the speed limit to two miles an hour, to which I'm getting the feeling this Council isn't gonna do."

Lucy scribbled her name on a chit, handed it to the City Clerk, and made her way back to the podium before Sheriff Vinson had finished handing out "Dare" bumper stickers to the Council members. "These Indian people," she began to drone, "don't care about our problems. They don't care about neighboring communities. Believe me, I used to live there. They didn't care about the voice of the people, or the average person who maybe didn't want to be an Indian all of a sudden, even if it did pay for re-chlorinating the municipal pool, which, if you look at the reports, is now so over-chlorinated, anyway, that it's a greater threat to the public health than the bacteria that they say they're eradicating, which I'm not sure of, and besides, if you actually read the literature, many of these bacteria are friendly —"

The egg timer again. Lucy had dreams where she smashed egg timers, called up the phone company time lady and hacked the machine so that the female automaton kept repeating the same hour and minute, and, in her most elaborate dream, she actually made time run backwards, got to filibuster in front of elected city officials until the universe had spun down to the moment right after the big bang. She'd wake up then, before seeing what would happen next, when time ran back right past the primal explosion. She wondered if people who had the benefit of a fine post-graduate education in physics ever had that dream and got to sleep long enough to see straight through to the end, that is, the beginning. But now she had to get to her point before the closing benediction was uttered.

"Okay, look, we can't handle this situation here by ourselves. This is what our representatives down in Albany are supposed to be doing for us. If you people cared about the future of this town, you'd be passing a resolution asking the state government to do something about that casino."

Lucy couldn't help herself. She was biting the hand that fed her three cats.

22
WASHINGTON, D.C.
APRIL 1999

Casey Elliott knew somebody. That person
knew somebody else, and that person knew
General Lucius Clay Adams, the new head
of the Army Corps of Engineers. He had
taken over with a mandate to keep the
agency, long involved in dam building, river
straightening, and other muscular engineer-
ing enterprises, from falling victim to the
new fashions in environmentalism. His
marching orders were outlined in a series of
interagency memos and a beautifully designed Web site: "Operation Change Focus
Quick." Where dams were now seen as the
enemy of a vibrant fishing industry, the
Corps would take on the task of destroying
the very structures it had once proudly
built; where flood-control projects had once
encased rivers in concrete straitjackets, the
Corps would now rip up the concrete and
restore riparian landscapes as good as, if
not better than, what nature had originally

provided. It was, General Adams confided to his staff, the same approach long taken by big-city construction unions: "Whether you're putting the shit up or tearing it down, as long as you're still getting paid, the system works."

So, when Casey used the BBU (Big Baby Underground) to reach General Adams, the reception was enthusiastic. Not just because the tall, soft-featured officer with the fine head of short-cropped red hair had, as he phrased it, "a hard-on for sticking it to the faggots at the Smithsonian," the whole nature of the project appealed to him. Daria Long's dream of the Native American Sculpture Park, the NASP, had been merged with Barbara Menzie's more lucrative vision of the Native American Hall of Fame. The combined attraction would, as Daria proposed, take shape on land that, up to now, had been the local wildlife refuge. Reclaiming such territory from the domain of the feral, clearing it, leveling it — that was the sort of thing the Corps could do with one bulldozer tied behind its back. The fact that the result would be an institution that would not only freeze out the candy-asses at the Smithsonian but garner PC brownie points for the Corps — well, sir, that was the frosting, the dressing, and the cake all rolled into one.

"So you'd what, move the wildlife in a truck to some other refuge or something?" Casey asked, in the same curious schoolboy tone he used for asking the planning commissioner whether the old Elks building could be razed for more casino parking.

"Shit no, Mr. Elliott, pardon my French fries, we just start blasting, and they find their own way out. They're crafty little suckers. That's why they call 'em wildlife."

Casey's green-of-center political sensibilities were slightly ruffled by the idea of "blasting" anything out, especially cute little — oh, you know, deer, deer ticks, whatever. "We are taking the chance that the blasting will kill some of the wildlife the preserve was originally set up to, you know, preserve, aren't we?"

"Mr. Elliott, I don't know you from Adam, except for our contacts through the BBU, but that fact alone tells me that you're no stranger to risk-taking. The sooner we sign off on this thing, the sooner paying customers will be rolling through your Hall of Fame, buying the souvenirs and snacks that are the lifeblood of any tourist operation. Now, the paperwork won't take you more than half an hour to burn through."

Filaquonsett Reservation, May 1999
"We are *live* at the site of the future Native American Hall of Fame and Sculpture Park, the NAHFSP, and the future this morning is at war with the past." Earlene Hammond was almost shouting into her microphone, but there was some yelling going on in the background, so the volume of her delivery wasn't quite as inexplicable to her listeners as what they had come to know as her pledge-drive-yowl. "There are about sixty environmental protestors from as far away as Poughkeepsie, and they have dared the Army Corps of Engineers bulldozers to roll over their currently prostrate bodies. Even if you haven't yet fulfilled your pledge, this is no time to touch that dial."

It wasn't that Earlene loved the sound of her own voice, like so many other people on the radio, the guys and gals who clearly, from the aural evidence, adore the tones they emit, even after they've sent those lovely vocal signals through the reverb, the compressor, the EQ, the shitty transmitter that had its last dose of real maintenance two years before the station was sold to Clear Channel. But she did love the pure

171

state of being on the air — the sheer adrenalizing power of being heard simultaneously by dozens, maybe even hundreds, of listeners.

More to the point, she didn't trust most of her volunteers to do anything more demanding than prerecord the announcements that she relentlessly cranked out on her computer — the promotions for upcoming shows, the funding credits that weren't really commercials for the sponsors who, on public radio, weren't really sponsors, the weather reports, the *Today in Tribal History* featurettes. When it came to live broadcasts, especially the anchoring of "breaking news" — usually just overly wordy introductions to the audio she stole from CNN by plugging an old Magnavox portable TV into the master control board — Earlene was The Voice of WQUO.

"As a matter of fact, almost all these protestors would appear to be from out of the reservation area. At the very least, we can say with certainty that none of them are faces I recognize from this station's annual Summerfest wine tastings, and, speaking of which, tickets for this year's Summerfest are very close to selling out, so if you do want to go, you should call us today and reserve your place."

The Greens, bearing signs that read "Save Nature, Not Face" and "Stop the Hall of Shame!" were, in fact, from out of town because none of the locals wanted to stand in the way of what was, in modern America, the most peculiar march of progress imaginable: the march backwards into the inglorious past of the Native Americans. Earlene described the protestors in careful, almost poetic detail, working in mentions of their headbands, their T-shirts, their sandals, and between descriptions she somehow managed to slide in persuasive reminders of Garrison Keillor's upcoming personal appearance. "He'll be signing CDs exclusively for our listeners," she proudly yelled.

At precisely twelve noon, tribal elder Barbara Menzies stepped to a podium and read a one-paragraph consecration of the site, which Anna Manybirds had crafted from shards of Oglala Sioux phrases. Earlene called it "strangely moving." Menzies then introduced Daria Long, resplendent in a black shift, who launched into a defense of the proposition that, since "we Native Americans revere nature like no other culture on the face of the planet," the Hall of Fame and Sculpture Park would, in fact, enhance visitors' appreciation of however much nature would survive the forthcoming temporary disruption. For every real hawk that might be displaced, Daria enthused, her hands fluttering over her head, there would be an abstract sculpture symbolizing all hawks.

Barbara, in her dealer's buckskin fringe, now waved a ceremonial flag ordered over the Internet from www.navajo.net. Then the large bulldozers farted great clouds of diesel smoke, emitted a joint rumble, and began advancing on nature's domain. The demonstrators held their ground until the machines had reached their shoes, at which point a senior demonstrator with a long gray ponytail and a "Ben & Jerry sold out" T-shirt blew a referee's whistle. The protestors scampered angrily to their feet and quickly re-formed as a circle dancing tauntingly around the bulldozers and chanting, "Shame!" The only injuries Earlene was able to discover for her wrap-up report on the day, "just before we join *Fresh Air,* already in progress," were two deer tick bites, one on a demonstrator and one on Barbara Menzies.

23
WOWOSA,
CONNECTICUT
JULY 1999

"It looks like Laverne is shtupping Shirley, doesn't it? See, *that's* a *'cute' "*. Joseph Catspaw was manipulating a couple of his most valuable TV-star collectibles in a clumsy simulation of fully clothed lesbian anal sex, partly for his own amusement, and partly to break the ice for his guest. "We're gonna do it our way from nowwww onnn!" Joseph sang as the girls bumped in rhythm. "Uh-oh," Joseph chuckled, "now it's Shirl's turn," and yes, the girls did swap places, and Joseph unstrapped the little miniature dildo from Laverne and refastened it on the dark-haired doll. Dick Stillwater sat on the other side of Joseph's massive mahogany desk, staring at the most goddamn peculiar dog-and-pony show he'd ever seen — and he'd both seen and given quite a few — and he wondered why he was here.

Bullshit, he knew why he was here. A guy

called Nighthawk or Nightwing or something had dug him out of a database of Northeastern New Yorkers with experience in government relations (damn small database, Dick thought as he gave his weave a nice paternal patting) and had called him up out of the blue, inviting him down to Wowosa for a, to use his term, "powwow."

Actually, Dick knew from a tirade delivered one night after one sherry too many by Dr. Roger Gardner, a night when the great educator actually unbuttoned his vest, "powwow" was one of those terrible clichés attributed to Native Americans (like "wampum" and "squaw") that bear no resemblance to any true NatAm lingo whatsoever. If you wanted to use an authentic Amerind word for a meeting, you'd invite a person down for a "caucus," but that word had actually been promoted into English, so it had lost its primitive cachet. But that linguistic insight didn't keep Dick Stillwater from hopping in his Jaguar XKE and bombing down the interstate to see what was up in the land of the competition. Little did he dream that what was up down there was a badly mimed bout of back-door intercourse by two miniaturized TV stars of the '70s.

"Look," Joseph said after the girls retired to their tiny powder room to freshen up, "it's stupid for the two of us to be, you should pardon the expression in this context, cannibalizing each other's businesses like this. We're an Indian casino, you're an 'Indian casino' — Joseph couldn't help putting air quotes around the second reference, couldn't quite bring himself to acknowledge the authenticity of the Filaquonsetts — "why should we beat each other up when we've both got common enemies, by which I mean the goombahs and schmucks of the world, the Donald Trumps and the Tony Silottas." Joseph looked to see if Dick betrayed some discomfort at the reference to the man Catspaw knew to be lurking behind the Filaquonsett curtain, but Dick just maintained his facade of tight-lipped smiling and barely noticeable nodding. "If we did coordinated marketing and government relations and public relations efforts," Joseph confided, trying to recapture his legendary ability to close a deal for ten gross of plus-size jeans with embroidered back pockets, "in no time at all we could make Atlantic Fucking City look like Pawtucket, Rhode Island, on a bad day in February."

"Joe, let me see if we're on the same page here," Dick oozed, relieved for the moment to be edging back toward paginational identity. "What you're suggesting is that we would merge those kinds of operations, but keep the backroom stuff totally separate?" Letting the Wowosans stick their noses under the tent, Dick knew, was bad enough, but letting them actually handle receipts — Tony Silotta would personally pour the concrete around his feet if Dick came back north and suggested that. Dick also wondered what Dr. Roger Gardner would think of the phrase "sticking their noses under the tent"; probably not an authentic Indian expression at all, he'd bet. Dr. Gardner had even pooh-poohed "teepee."

"Yeah, sure, if that floats your boat," Joseph said, and Dick could swear that the man across the desk winked at him. Pretty shameless, winking at an old winker. "We could both contribute to an advertising-marketing-govrelations kitty, and those funds would represent the only commingling. Except for my girls here."

"Well, you know, I'd have to run everything by the Council of Elders," Dick cooed in what he hoped was a voice of sweet reason.

"Yeah" — Joseph couldn't avoid just a soupcon of sarcasm — "the Elders."

"But, you know" — Dick took a chance here, thinking, what the fuck, this guy's so focused on his little dolls — "we're having some vandalism problems up there, so that's probably the first thing on our agenda, tightening up security, making sure our visitors get the full Filaquonsett experience without having a brick land in their fucking lap."

"Are you kidding me?" Joseph inquired with the utmost innocence. "Who would try to vandalize you guys? Who would be so dumb as to mess with a goddamn Indian tribe?" At this point, he maneuvered the Laverne doll back on top of his desk. "Hello!" he singsonged as she sashayed toward Dick. "I know that's not Laverne's line," Joseph Catspaw explained apologetically, "but I had to sell my Squiggy doll to pay for my wife's last nose job. She wanted more pert."

24
Manhattan,
New York
July 1999

"That's fine, Socorro, thank you," Reeny Silotta singsonged at her Guatemalan housekeeper. Serena didn't actually know any Spanish, but she fancied that the strange melody she adopted when she talked to her maid got close enough to the way "they" talked to make it more understandable to the help than Vegas English. Sure enough, Socorro, muttering, "Yes, missus," retreated to the kitchen. Serena smiled proudly at her dinner guests, Vince and Eileen Winstanley, and cocked her head at the retreating short, dark, stocky figure in the white uniform. "She makes the best pasta primavera this side of Stardust Boulevard. She swears there's no cream in it, but Tony says it tastes like there's half a cow in there. Please, start."

"Speaking of Tony, shouldn't we wait for him?" Eileen asked, and Serena waved off the idea as if Art Bell had suggested waiting for the arriving party of Martians. "Well, I want to make sure he gets a look at those paintings before I have to ship them back," Eileen said warily. "That's a pretty fine collection we're being offered — the Dogfood-dot-com people pretty much invested their entire last IPO in buying art for their offices."

"Mmm," Reeny uttered in a simulation of interest, filtered through a mouthful of fusilli.

"And they don't have any offices anymore, so we're talking about a very motivated seller."

They were seated in the dining room of the Silottas' Central Park West apartment, a place Tony had bought because Serena was tired of staying at hotels when she came to New York to shop. The apartment was decorated, under Serena's personal supervision, in Tony's favored style: ultra-pretentious neo-classical. There were white Corinthian columns, non-weight-bearing, in the kitchen. Plaster Cupids and *Thinkers* were strewn through the living and dining rooms, and a *David,* two-fifths' sized (though, at Tony's insistence, with "the actual-size penis, for Christ's sake, that's what it's all about") stood at the foot of the blue-silk-canopied bed. The only other

181

David replicas of comparable size in this country were at Caesar's Palace and Forest Lawn.

"So, Serena" — Eileen was paddling the conversation as hard as she could while Vince watched from the shoreline — "how come you stopped dancing? Don't you ever miss it?"

"Yeah, I miss it. But Tony prefers me to maintain a more respectable profile as his wife. He built me a stage in our house in Vegas, and there's a band on call, so I can still do the old numbers whenever I get the urge. Of course, without the rest of the girls and no audience, the vibe's a little different . . ."

As Socorro padded in with the main course, a Dover sole wrapped in a thin potato crust and served with tomato coulis ("Best tomato coulis on the Upper West Side," Serena announced), Mrs. Tony Silotta began her assigned task for the evening. "So, kids, it looks like Tony's running a little late. Vince, you've had the opportunity to see how The Silotta Organization treats its employees — you've been happier than a pig in shit, right, Eileen?"

Eileen, prim and thin-lipped, smart and proper, was very glad she had a mouthful of Dover sole at that moment, since the mood

182

of our porcine friends in ordure had never before been a topic of her dinnertime conversation. Vince, sensing that he was the subject at hand anyway, gallantly stepped in. "Eileen has never been happier since she left graduate school, married me, and entered into the fabulous world of Interior Department cocktail parties. We got two new Great Danes —"

"Yich. You like them? They're killers, aren't they?" Serena whined.

"Actually," Eileen had recovered enough to take over at this slight to the Winstanleys' shared passion, "they're the nicest dogs in the world. They're smart, they're playful —"

"If something that big is gonna play with me, it better be a linebacker with a Super Bowl ring," Serena countered, ending the dog conversation.

"We raise them and show them at —" Vince offered, but Serena held up her right hand, the endless nails painted a shiny kelly green, and moved right ahead. "So, look, Vince, I think Tony's very fond of your family. You know, we're family people, we like to keep things family. So Tony was kind of wondering if you'd like to join The Silotta Organization —"

"Or family," Vince suggested. He saw immediately that whatever else he and Serena

183

might have in common, a sense of humor was not in the inventory. "What kind of —"

Reeny cut him off like a Ford Expedition sideswiping a Neon. "Tony thinks that the Filaquonsett operation is gonna be getting some heavy pressure on the governmental level, and he thinks that nobody in the tribe has the expertise in, you know, that thing."

"That government thing."

"Yeah. Hey, there's pie for —"

Serena's cell phone piped up, playing the song she used to close with, "The Main Event." "Uh-huh. Yeah. Here." She handed the phone, tiny as a promise, a fashion accessory you could talk into, to Vince.

"Hello?"

"So?" It was Tony. Vince heard some noise in the background. It sounded like a man moaning.

"Well, I'm not quite sure what —"

"Look, you know what lobbyists do, you know how they do it, and I'm sure you know they get paid a fuck of a lot better than G-15s at the Bureau of Indian Affairs, am I right?"

"Well, I'm actually a G-18, but —"

"Look, I'm sorry I couldn't be there with you, Christopher Cross's manager didn't think I could count the number of years since his client had a hit record, and I had to walk his internal organs through some remedial math. What do you say?"

"Maybe I should talk it over with Eileen . . ."

"She told me she thought you'd be great."

"Pie?" Serena offered sweetly. Vince rubbed his head, forgetting that it was no longer a crew cut, so he now looked as if he'd just gotten out of bed. "No thanks. To the pie, Tony. To you? I guess — I mean, mainly stuff in Albany?"

"Mainly wherever people in government have a beef with Native American people trying to make an honest living. We'll talk money when I get back. Don't be an idiot, have some pie."

Vince had had two glasses of an Italian chardonnay so he couldn't be sure, but he thought that out of the corner of his eye he saw *The Thinker* wink at him.

25
FILAQUONSETT
RESERVATION
AUGUST 1999

Dr. Roger Gardner was proudly striding through the hallway of the Chatting Eagle Conference Center at the Filaquonsett Casino, every wavy gray hair plastered into shining place, every button on the 46 portly black Botany 500 three-piece with the most subtle striping imaginable buttoned to the hilt. The conference center had been his idea, the premise being that, all other things being equal, businessmen would prefer to have their meetings and conventions in a lovely place where they were treated like kings about to piss away their ransoms. But nothing made him prouder than to have persuaded the NAGA convention to meet at the Big F, as he liked to call it. NAGA was the Native American Gaming Association, the trade association for Indian casinos. Dr. Gardner's previous contribution to the organization's welfare was convincing it, the previous year, to change its name from the National Native American Gaming Association, on the premise that its acronym, NNAGA, sounded like someone was, as he delicately phrased it, experiencing reverse peristalsis.

Walking with him, trying to keep up, actually, with Dr. Gardner's furiously purposeful pace, was a tall, slender, amazingly pale-faced executive with the Five Crowns hotel chain. Dr. Gardner had forgotten his name, and the guy was too proud of his chocolate brown Hugo Boss suit to wear the name tag where you could see it, but the point was that here was someone just drooling at the idea of turning the old post office building into a four-and-a-half-star hotel. "What we at Five Crowns like about dealing with Indian people — excuse me, Native American people," the guy tut-tutted while Dr. Gardner smiled to indicate no sensitivity on that score, "is that you've got this sovereignty thing, so you can fast-track the shit out of a project. You know, most places we want to do a hotel and/or hotel-resort property, the interest we pay while waiting for their local whoozis and whatsis to sign off on the thing, that could pay for enough extra soundproofing to make the place fully five-star."

Dr. Gardner nodded. He'd learned to

curb his natural tendency to expostulate — what his ex-wife cruelly called pontificate, though he had nothing but respect for those who knew less than he did — since the people who wanted to do business on tribal lands these days tended to sell themselves on the idea. All you had to do was nod solemnly from time to time, as if in recognition of the deep tribal wisdom that was on the verge of blessing the deal.

"But I do have a talk to deliver, so let's meet for drinks," Dr. Gardner said, clasping ol' what's-his-name on the shoulder as if they were long-separated army buddies, then sharply increasing his pace away from the guy.

The talk was a triumph. "Customs Make Customers" was the title, and Dr. Roger Gardner had gathered both statistics and anecdotes to prove that, when people were deciding where to go to gamble, the presence of artifacts, cultural activities, or artistic touches could tip the balance in favor of Native American casinos. "Folks feel guilty enough about indulging in gaming," Dr. Gardner said, narrating a section of the speech illustrated with large-screen PowerPoint graphs of Frank Luntz polling data commissioned by the Filaquonsett Nation. "We have a great gift to offer the white man. We can give him permission to leave more at our tables and in our machines simply through giving him the added value of a cultural experience," he intoned. "If you've got dancers in your community, why not place them at strategic spots all through the facility, especially near food-service areas. If you've got painters, give them a little spot in the elevator lobby, where there's usually enough light for them. Music? Native American chants and songs sound great when you're putting your callers on hold." They didn't give standing O's at NAGA conferences — that was the white man's way — but the buzz in the room after Dr. Gardner finished his talk was electric enough to run Ed Begley Jr.'s house for a year.

"Well, you know, my strong suit has always been education," Dr. Roger Gardner was saying now, in the Bark 'n' Brew Lounge, to his friend from the Five Crowns, who was drooling admiration for the speech, especially its brevity. "In that field, you get in, impart the knowledge you want to inject, and get the hell out before you bore people to tears." Above their heads, a bank of television screens all carried silent images

— sports highlights unreeling on ESPN, Geraldo Rivera arguing with lawyers on the Fox News Channel.

"Well, as I was saying, we're very high on this whole Indian thing," Five Crowns said as he downed a Coors, "and as far as the cultural stuff you were talking about, it sounded just great, but, and I just want to double-check my memory here, none of it would be mandatory, would it?"

Dr. Gardner produced his best hail-fellow-well-met hearty laugh, the one he had learned by watching Dick Stillwater at work. It was the response he now resorted to whenever he was tempted, in a professional conversation, to scream, "You fucking idiot, didn't you hear a goddamn word I just said?" at his conversational partner. For others, possessed of lesser intellects, perhaps the studied guffaw offered a chance to think of an appropriate retort. But for Roger Gardner, who thought faster than fruit flies mate, it was just an opportunity to maintain the even-tempered surface he knew was essential in his new Filaquonsett identity. He had never, in the months since tribalization, seen one real Native American who was sober scream the words "you fucking idiot" at anyone.

He was about to recover from the laugh,

to point out to Five Crowns in the gentlest, wisest possible way that the "cultural stuff" was exactly the heart of the point he was making, when Daria Long ran into the lounge, spotted him, and made what you could call a beeline for him, assuming the bee was short, stout, middle-aged, and had a bad knee from spinning class. "It's the NAHFSP," she wheezed, but she was also crying, in tears now that her long-dreamed-of sculpture park might be further delayed, or scuttled altogether. The Corps of Engineers bulldozers were her engines of vindication, a noisy, fume-spewing rebuke to all the local doubters who had laughed at her dream, all the philistines in feathers who wouldn't understand art if it moved into their house and started using their kitchen.

She pulled herself together enough to pour out an explanation. "Somebody got to the state government, they've sent snow-blowers out here to stop our bulldozers. All the Council of Elders members are in the sweat lodge, and there's a 'Do Not Disturb' sign on the door. You've got to do something." Dr. Roger Gardner put that old-friend clasp on Five Crowns's shoulder again and followed Daria out through the casino, while over their heads, Judge Judy

silently heaped contempt on a hapless de-
fendant.

26
FILAQUONSETT
RESERVATION
AUGUST 1999

It was true. There in the muggy afternoon sun stood a dozen snowblowers from the New York State Department of Land Resources, forming a silent circle around the parked Corps of Engineers bulldozers. The 'dozer drivers sat in their cabs, eating sandwiches, playing their radios louder even than do the kids who pay three grand just for the subwoofers in their SUVs. Country music from the 'dozers, mostly, Shania Twain's voice bouncing off the trees, along with some hip-hop — Dr. Roger Gardner counted twenty "fucks" just as he stood there with Daria and assessed the situation.

"It's terrible, Roger. Somebody doesn't want the Native American Hall of Fame and Sculpture Park to happen," Daria wailed.

"A lot of people didn't want it to happen, Daria, I was at the meetings," Dr. Gardner shouted in his most reassuring tenor, over the battle between black and white music.

"This is something else. This is war on a fine Indian nation."

I am a man of thought, Dr. Roger Gardner thought to himself, but this is a time for action. Leaving Daria to stare at the standoff between the giant machines, Dr. Gardner strutted over to the driver of one of the snowblowers.

Daria kept her gaze on Dr. Gardner. He was not her favorite member of the Filaquonsett tribe, it's true — she had never even thought of inviting him over for schnitzel. But she did have to admire the way he just walked right up to a big, tattooed redneck who could probably pop him one right in the schnoz and lay him out flat cold. She saw him engage in what he'd probably call spirited dialogue with the 'blower driver, Dr. Gardner even having the spine to waggle a pedantic finger in the man's face. The guy replied curtly, with what looked to Daria like a bit of a snarl. This was not going to end, she thought, with Dr. Gardner maintaining vertical.

Suddenly, the great man spun on his heels, and trotted back in the direction of the casino, turning over his shoulder just to give Daria a thumbs-up. Either he'd made surprising progress, she mused, or he really did like her, despite her recent weight gain.

Daria stood there in the pale afternoon sun, listening to the battle of the radio bands and worrying about all the splendid and important artworks she'd commissioned that might never get to be installed on this hallowed spot: Eleanor Peoria's amazing *Wig Warm,* a seventy-two-by-sixteen-foot web of heated stainless-steel tubes, each junction of which was topped by a wig depicting a different Native American hairstyle; Jürgen Volk's massive *Big Red Man,* a three-story-high statue drawing on visual elements of both Crazy Horse and Chief Dan George, built completely out of petrified buffalo jerky; *Blanket,* a work by the Memory Collective of the Sandia tribe, a massive evocation of the smallpox-tainted blankets handed out by the U.S. Army to Native Americans built out of stainless steel and painted black.

All of these works were controversial in their own way: Some people thought the wigs were insulting; others objected to the fact that Volk was a German living in Leipzig; and still others, true philistines, said the so-called blanket looked more like a giant black garbage can that had been run over and flattened by a fleet of Jeeps. Daria had fought for all of them through acrimonious Tribal Arts Council meetings. And now none of them might ever see the light of northern New York day. It was too much for the gallant avatar of all things artistic. The short, stout, middle-aged woman with the curly brown hair started heaving in sobs, oddly in time to the beats of Mystikal booming from one of the 'dozers.

And then Dr. Roger Gardner was strolling, cockier than a tinhorn despot, back toward the 'blower driver, obviously the leader of their crew. He exchanged a few words with the big lug, and then handed to him through the driver's window a paper bag. It looked heavy to Daria. Was Dr. Gardner trying to bribe these men with sandwiches? Why hadn't she thought of that? Before she could do a mental inventory of her fridge, the 'blower driver gave a high-sign out his window to his colleagues, the snowblowers started up their engines, and within five minutes the bulldozers stood triumphant, their enemies creeping back down the highway, metaphorical tails between their metaphorical legs.

Daria watched as Dr. Roger Gardner did his home-run trot back to join her, his lips pressed together in a toothless grin of determined victory. "What did you give them?" she asked in a still-tremulous voice.

Dr. Gardner looked at her with the kind of smug satisfaction he would feel explaining gravity to Newton, but spoke only one word. "Chips," he said.

27
SCOTTSDALE, ARIZONA
AUGUST 1999

The clicking had stopped permanently. Hap Matthews had gotten some new teeth. He'd stayed retired in Scottsdale, Arizona, only long enough to realize that doing something as badly as he played golf was not a particularly amusing way to spend his silver years. Just at that point, the years began to get golden.

The opportunity had come, he told his wife, Lucille, to "monetize my experience at Interior." Monetize was not a word in Hap's own vocabulary, it came from the conversation he had with a gentleman he didn't know but who seemed to know a lot about Hap, a gentleman who phoned the house one day and suggested a stroll on such a fine spring morning out at the Pavilion Lakes Country Club. "I'm starting to hate golf," Hap said to the mysterious gentleman. "I know," the voice on the phone answered.

The gentleman turned out to be a dapper guy in his late fifties, a full head of shining black hair, a face like a particularly smooth Ambrosia melon, a body like a torpedo, wearing a *Sopranos* crew jacket and a pair of khaki trousers. As the desert sun started to bake the greens, he led Hap on a tour of the part of the course Hap had never visited before — the periphery, far from the flags and fairways, out where the high green fence kept errant golf balls from sailing into the windows of the tack shops, the boot shops, and the Fendi and Prada and Louis Vuitton boutiques in the adjoining upscale mall. "I know somebody on the *Sopranos* crew," the gentleman confided with a wicked grin, "and he thought I'd get a kick out of this." It was the only piece of personal information he shared with Hap Matthews.

His proposition was straightforward: Hap would use his connections in the Interior Department to derail the "whole Filaquonsett deal" any way he knew how. Hap had to admit his memory was a little dim on whatever that deal was, that's why you have underlings, but the gentleman filled him in. In exchange for this little bit of help, he and Lucille (how the hell does this guy know her name?) could become regular, very valued, customers at every single one of those fine stores in the upscale mall. Hell, if they wanted to, they could buy the freaking mall. Best of all, it would be cash money, a little tax-free retirement fund for a guy who'd given so much to his country and gotten so damned little back. The gentleman seemed to know Hap very well.

It was getting stupidly hot. They shook hands and parted strangers.

Washington, D.C., October 1999
"Interesting to see you here, Hap," Vince Winstanley said in an excess of understatement.

"Hey — " Hap smiled, showing more teeth than Vince remembered — "gotta be somewhere. And you are?"

"Representing the Filaquonsetts," Vince smiled, pointing an index finger at the subtle hawk pin on his lapel.

It struck Vince, sitting in the front row of chairs facing the dais in Room H447 at Interior Department headquarters, that his retired ex-boss was not there just to show off his new choppers. "You testifying in favor of the tribe?" Vince gently probed.

" 'Fraid not, old pal. For the first time since I dinged your request for a larger travel budget, we appear to be on opposing sides." Retirement, Vince thought, had taken some of the bureaucratic caution out of his old boss. The guy's demeanor was fearless, almost swaggering. Also, his suit was nicer than anything Vince remembered from the Hap Matthews collection. "I don't know whether you're aware of this, but that so-called tribe of yours is a sham. They're going to be de-recognized, they are going *down*," Hap informed his former underling. "Also — " he now decided to plunge the knife in up to the hilt — "you're a little too old to be growing your hair out, my friend. How's Eileen?"

Their conversation, such as it was, was interrupted by a sound from the hallway outside Room H447 that was clearly not the polite chattering of lobbyists on their way into a tribal recognition review hearing. It sounded like angry chanting. Vince thought it sounded vaguely . . . *Lakota.*

The mahogany doors to the room swung open, and in rushed several hundred war-painted people. War paint on their faces, but jeans and T-shirts (sporting such slogans as "Just Do It" and "This Bud's For You") identifying them as members of the tribe of Native American young people. Boys and girls in their teens and twenties suddenly filled the room with the sound of their chanting as they squatted, arms linked, in the aisles and in the narrow gap between the dais and the front row of seats. Frantic gaveling from Hap Matthews's successor, an Interior Department lifer named Emmet Saulls, finally succeeded in getting the noise down sufficiently that Saulls could lean into the microphone and get the words "Let's just come to some kind of order here . . ." out into the PA before a striking young woman made her way to the front of the chanting group.

She had long black hair in symmetrical shiny braids, blazing brown eyes, and the morning's uniform of jeans and a T-shirt. Her shirt said "Remember Wounded Knee." Her jeans said "Old Navy."

She spoke in an unamplified but clear, loud, sharp voice. "My name is Jennifer New Moon, and I have come with a delegation of Lakota Sioux people to say you have no right to conduct today's hearing. A Native American tribe is a sovereign nation, and has no obligation to respond to the political tricks of the white man."

Hap Matthews gave a series of little facial tics and gestures in the direction of the chairman's seat, and Vince Winstanley couldn't help wondering if, in retirement, his old supervisor had begun to develop a case of Tourette's. Or, Vince got a little more charitable in his thoughts, maybe he's just volunteering as a third-base coach in a Scottsdale Little League team. In fact, Hap was desperately trying to cue, to prompt his successor to get back to the point. Finally, Emmet Saulls's dead gray eyes flickered with a dim spark of recognition, and he spoke up.

"Young lady, this panel believes that it is in possession of credible information that the so-called Filaquonsett Nation is, in fact, a totally fictional entity, and we're holding this evidentiary hearing to —" He never got the end of his sentence out of his impossibly thin-lipped mouth. The words were drowned by the noise of the young Native Americans banging on small, feather-trimmed drums. Emmet Saulls looked helplessly at Hap, who turned to Vince. "Friends of yours?" he asked, cocking his head toward the chanting, drumming youngsters. Vince shrugged. "Jackpot winners," he whispered, amused in spite of himself. "I hear we've got very loose slots."

Finally, after enough drumming to infuriate the regulars at an Ibiza disco, Jennifer put her right hand up, and the room grew silent. "It is no longer time for the white man to tell us who is, and who is not, one of us. It is we who will define ourselves. For hundreds of years, the white man slaughtered us. Now, if some of his number wish to join us, we welcome them. Today," she said, her voice rising to a tone she hoped was noble and determined, but actually sounded more like a teenage girl shrieking in disappointment that her Gap store was sold out of skimpy turquoise tops in her size, "today we are all Filaquonsetts!" The room erupted in chants and cheers.

Hap Matthews shrugged and shot a shit-eating grin at the dais, and Emmet Saulls gaveled the hearing to an indefinite recess. "Want to have some lunch, for old times' sake?" Vince inquired as Hap gathered up his Louis Vuitton briefcase and his black Armani raincoat. It was a specious question. Hap had never in his career lunched with underlings, but Vince was trying to be a gracious winner.

"No thanks," Hap said as he started to step over the swaying, chanting New Filaquonsetts. "I might as well save a guy some trouble. I'm gonna go home and shatter my own kneecaps."

28
FILAQUONSETT
RESERVATION
NOVEMBER 1999

"Two years ago, Elena Hawkwing was unemployed. Out of work. Out of hope. Then, something happened to change all that. Now, she sees a future bright with promise. All because of — a *casino*." It was a deep voice, not scary-deep like the voice that threatened two hours of bloodcurdling thrills at a new summer movie, but warm-fireplace-and-cozy-slippers deep, morning-in-America deep, like the voice that told you how nice the Citibank folks would be if you asked them for a loan. A piano picked out a melody that built from distressed minor to hopeful major, and strings lingered solici-tously in the background. "Don't let the enemies of hope take the future away from Elena Hawkwing," the voice urged. "Don't let them close the Filaquonsett Casino . . . the House of Hope."

"Lights." Tony Silotta barked, and, as the

lights in the meeting room came up, Barbara Menzies could be seen dabbing at her eyes with a tissue. It was the first time she'd cried since the "Ellen Comes Out" episode aired. "Now that spot, which cost us a cool two million to shoot, will be airing in all New York State TV markets," Tony said, looking at Dick Stillwater to make sure he had all the television mumbo-jumbo straight, "with especially heavy runs in the Albany area, which assumes that our distinguished state legislators turn on the TV after they've sent the hookers home." Some of the members of the Council of Elders chuckled at Tony's jibe at the lawmakers, although Barbara Menzies shot him a dark look through the tail end of her tears.

"Tony?" Curtis Zorn piped up. "This is a great, great commercial, and I think I speak for everybody on the Council of Elders in saying that it's an excellent piece of work, and that, of course, casino revenues will pay for the production of the piece."

"But?" Tony interrupted, knowing that Curtis was just laying some long-winded pipe before finally getting around to turning on a faucet of hot bullshit.

"But, you know, this is kind of a small community and/or tribe, and I've canvassed my colleagues here and, hard as it may be to believe this, not a single one of us knows this Elena Hawkwing. Could you possibly —"

"Jesus fucking Christ, pardon me, I know this is a small town, but you still don't have to ride shotgun in the turnip truck, do you? Are you kidding me? What, am I talking to total mouth-breathers here?" The last was addressed to Dick Stillwater, who shrugged and pantomimed back an answer that looked a lot like, "Maybe not total mouth breathers, but . . ."

"Of course you don't know Elena Hawkwing. You know why? Because I made her the fuck up. The only way you'd know her is if you'd been at the casting sessions in Queens a week ago Tuesday. Let me lay it all out for the late bloomers in the room, okay? This is television. We could put Council of Elders member Menzies on the screen, pardon me, and the absolutely only thing we'd influence in the entire New York State area is the sales of Imodium."

Barbara Menzies shot Tony another dark look, this time from entirely dry eyes. Tony stared right back. He'd seen tougher-looking lesbians draped over Reeny backstage. "We're in a war here, people. What I'm saying to you is that not only do we have to make Elena Hawkwing the most beloved

New Yorker since . . . I don't know, Joe fucking Namath, we've got to get involved in the political process in a big way, we've got to contribute to the campaigns of every stiff in Albany who either has been or could be a friend of ours, because you know for a pig-fucking fact that our opposition is putting a royal shit-load of money into the hands of legislators who want to see this whole tribe turned back into just another bunch of poor-ass white people. That's the name of that tune." Tony sat down, as drained as if he'd just sung two hour-long sets of wild uptempo standards with the swingin' Johnny Pantoleone Orchestra.

Casey Elliott was letting his long, greasy, black hair hang down below his shoulders at Council of Elders meetings these days, giving him nothing to do with his hands when he felt fidgety. After what seemed to everybody else in the room like a thoughtful pause but was just Casey checking to make sure that nothing was amiss in the downstairs department, he stood up. "Tony's brought us this far," he said, his voice quavering slightly.

"And?" Barbara Menzies asked.

"And . . . I just thought we should keep in mind that Tony's brought us this far."

Barbara Menzies sighed into her microphone so heavily that Steve, the board operator back at WQUO, sprang up from his semi-nap, convinced by what sounded like a burst of white noise that the phone line to the meeting had been lost. He was reassured a moment later by the familiar sound of the gooseneck creaking, as Barbara pushed the mike away from her face for the moment it took to avoid calling Casey, a lifelong political ally of hers, a brain-dead hippie. Having thus regained her composure, Barbara swung the mike back in front of her freshly lipsticked mouth and fixed her gaze at the podium in the center of the chamber, at Tony Silotta.

"Mr. Silotta, just for the record here tonight, who would these opponents of ours be? I mean, we've made this commercial, we seem to have committed ourselves to some kind of a battle here, based on just a few indications that not everybody in the world likes our little tribe, but —"

"Council of Elders member Menzies," Tony uttered the phrase slowly, the disdain blanketing each word like tepid hollandaise on room-service Benedict, "have you ever heard of Wowosa? Have you ever heard of organized crime? Do I have to draw you, pardon my language, a fucking picture?"

The hotline rang at the control room of

WQUO, and Steve's second attempt at a nap was spoiled. Earlene was calling, having been listening to the station while rereading some Kerouac. "Listen to me. This is urgent. This could lose us our license. You get the agendas of the Council of Elders, don't you?" Not waiting for an answer, she plowed right ahead. "The very next time this man, this Mr. Silotta is scheduled to testify, you make absolutely, one hundred percent sure we're on seven-second delay."

29
WASHINGTON, D.C.
NOVEMBER 1999

Dr. Roger Gardner was dying to scratch. The elk-fur vest he was wearing over his Turnbull & Asser shirt itched worse than anything he'd experienced since his episode of adult-onset chicken pox, but he knew better than to indicate discomfort with an article of his tribal garb. This was serious business he was engaged in, and a little itching was a small price to pay for the survival of a way of life.

He and his new live-in companion, the ethnically lovely and ethnically talented Anna Manybirds, had flown to Washington, D.C., to testify at a recognition hearing for a would-be Native American tribe in Uppland County, the Meshtinguotts. Anna had moved in with Dr. Gardner the previous winter, when it appeared she might be about to return to southern Alaska. Dr. Gardner, so taken with this woman who could do the Eagle Dance and finish it up with a ridicu-

211

lously fine bout of oral sex, invited her to move in to his historic residence. Anna, who had come to appreciate white men's ways since arriving in the former community of Gammage, particularly admired Dr. Gardner's sense of authority, his way with words, his willingness to be more chiefly than so many of the modern white men she had met. "You'll live like no Tlingit ever has, or ever will," he promised her, "unless they get with the program and open a casino."

And now she sat proudly in the front row, a necklace of eagle beaks sparkling against the size 12 Donna Karan coatdress from the Beaver Plaza Mall right inside the atrium of the Big F, as Dr. Gardner testified against federal recognition of this new tribe. "I recognize that, as a representative of a nation so recently acknowledged, it may seem odd for me to be opposing this petition," Dr. Gardner conceded, "but it's my sad duty to point out that, according to the information we have, this so-called tribe is nothing more than a front for the organized-crime gambling interests that feel threatened by the Filaquonsett success. Their goal is to flood northeastern New York State with casinos, with traffic, with demands upon public services and infrastructure and, while they reap the profits, they also return our tribe to its previous state of penury." He locked on Chairman Emmet Saulls's eyes, which seemed particularly blank. At length, Dr. Gardner took pity on the man. "The opposite of prosperity," he said helpfully.

Two hours later, Anna Manybirds was back on their bed at the Four Seasons, aimlessly browsing through the cable menu, trying to find something to watch, wondering to herself why, at this late stage of Native American prosperity, there was not yet a cable channel dedicated to the tribal nations. Dr. Roger Gardner had delayed his return to their suite in order to pick up some Altoids at the gift shop, but events sometimes have a way of interfering with even the most mundane purchases. So instead of indulging in some needed breath-refreshment on the power-walk upstairs to his Tlingit love nest, he was now riding in the backseat of a black Lincoln Town Car, restrained by the presence of two Samoan fullbacks who flanked him and looked ready, he thought unsteadily, to kill and eat him. A voice from the front seat, piped through a tinny speaker behind him, was all he knew of his other driving companion or companions, since the heavily smoked privacy screen between front and back was all the way up.

"You think your friend Mr. Silotta is not in, quote, organized crime?"

Dr. Gardner paused at this question, then he made his first mistake. "Unquote," he couldn't help himself from saying.

"What do you think this is, a fucking English lesson?"

"No, sir, I think it's an attempt at intimidation. And I don't believe that Mr. Silotta is in organized anything. Just organizing his wife would seem to be a full-time job. Such a charge, I would think, just amounts to ethnic stereotyping, and, as a Native American —"

On some unseen or unheard signal, perhaps coming through their little white earpieces, the two Samoans smartly elbowed Dr. Roger Gardner in the ribs, in stereo. He didn't just have the wind knocked out of him; it felt as if he'd had the lungs knocked out of him. Doubled over, he had what he recognized was not, in the present circumstances, a useful thought: The damn vest still itched.

"Listen, my friend. How do you think this is gonna end? The little guy wins? David beats Goliath? Is that how you think this goes? You see, your friend Mr. Silotta did something only pimply faced teenagers are supposed to do. He ran away from home.

That's right. He thinks he can be a lone wolf in the gaming business and step on the toes of some nice people who used to be his family. Well, David, check back in with me in a few minutes, let me know how you like sharing a ride with a couple of Goliaths."

The voice clicked off its microphone, and the car sped out past Reagan National Airport into suburban Virginia. Again as if on cue, each Samoan delivered an open-handed slap to one side of Dr. Roger Gardner's head, a matched set of blows that immediately gave him a front-row seat at the world's loudest carillon concert. But, at least, right at that moment, the vest didn't itch so much anymore.

Filaquonsett Reservation, November 1999
"From this next moon on . . ." Ricky Coelho sang. "Youuu and I, babe, like the hawk, we fly soo high, babe, from this next moon onnnnnn . . ." Ricky was casting his spell in Club Suit, the state-of-the-art concert theater of the Big F, and Curtis Zorn and his wife, Sandy, were soaking in it. Ricky was known as "the Native American Sinatra," and his show was a fast-paced revue of Sinatra favorites, with just a touch of Shoshone thrown in, narrated in the first person, with biographical details ("Hey, I

215

just married this swingin' chick, Ava Gardner. Ring a ding ding!") sprinkled throughout the set in an order that was dizzily unchronological. Ricky paced around the stage in a Sinatra-esque tux, with an elaborate feathered headdress setting it off, and the cigarette he used as a Chairman of the Board-type prop was actually herbal. His big closer, of course, was "New York, New York," where what melted away were "these little tribe blues."

Curtis was having a rough day. Anna Manybirds, in tears in her tub-cum-Jacuzzi, had wailed over the phone that Dr. Roger Gardner was nowhere near the gift shop. Vince Winstanley had reported in via e-mail from Albany that the State Legislature was considering at least half a dozen bills, each of which activated a different, cleverly quasi-legal method of, as Vince put it, "taxing the Filaqunsettts down the toity." Vince reluctantly leaned toward the belief that only baskets full of legal tender could solve the problem. And, to top things off, his wife, Sandy, had insisted they come to see Ricky Coelho, who, to Curtis's ear, sounded like Frank Sinatra Jr. with a cold, a cough, and a slight Oklahoma accent. As usual, he strove to find the good in his situation. "Boy," he said to Sandy, "if you didn't see there was just a guy with a synthesizer and a drummer on the stage, you'd swear there was a whole five-piece band up there." She nodded dreamily.

After the show, Curtis spent a quarter-hour waiting for Sandy to consume her nonfat cap at The Roasting Beaver (Tony's idea, an actual coffee roasting machine in the casino's shopping court — "It fills the place with a great smell, and the customers pay for it"). The chief's day was about to put itself out of its misery when he saw something in front of the casino out on Revered Ancestors' Way (formerly Elm Street) that chilled his blood.

Usually, members of the Council of Elders didn't socialize outside meetings and the pre-meetings where they decided what would happen in the meetings, so Curtis didn't keep up with the changing lifestyles of the other community leaders. His first thought on seeing the man with the four multicolored parrots sitting on his head and shoulders in front of the casino was, Jesus, those things must peck like crazy. His second thought, as his political conscious-ness flickered back to life, was, Those poor birds are probably endangered species from a habitat that's being wiped out in the rain forest. And the third thought was, That

217

moron who's standing out here offering his birds for photos sitting on Casino tourists — the big red mynah was right now perched uneasily on the shoulder of a young black girl giggling as she tried to keep the bird from eating her dreads — is fucking Casey Elliott!

"Casey!" Chief Curtis Zorn shouted over the traffic noise as soon as the red mynah had returned to his home perch and started gnawing at Casey's ponytail. "What the hell are you doing?"

"Hey, Chief."

"Knock off the 'hey, Chief' shit. You're a member of the governing body of the tribe. Don't you think this is a little . . . trailer-park?" Curtis hissed at him.

"I saw a couple of guys doing this on the main drag in Waikiki and, just like they told me, you can make a bundle with these lil' guys. It's great color for the casino, and it's much more lucrative than telephone sales. And, no, I don't think it's trailer-park. As a matter of fact, hi, Sandy, don't give him your finger, he'll bite it off, as a matter of fact, I remember when you'd think a phrase like 'trailer-park' was more than a little elitist, my friend."

"Listen, Casey, you can't pull that lefter-than-thou stuff with me. Wait in the car, honey. We're running a multimillion-dollar operation here, and we've got big-time friends, and big-time enemies. Standing out on the street with parrots —"

"Two of them are mynahs, and the blue one's a lorikeet," Casey corrected.

"How did you get them here?"

"There's a guy brings them in. It's exceedingly legal."

"Doesn't have much to do with Native American culture or anything, though, does it?"

Casey shrugged, something that took a lot of effort with a good-sized tropical bird on each shoulder. It was late enough, and the traffic had dropped off enough, that Curtis thought he heard an odd sloshing kind of sound as Casey made the gesture. "How was the Sinatra guy?"

Now it was Curtis's turn to shrug. As he turned to join Sandy in their late-model Saab, it occurred to him there was no sloshing when he shrugged.

Northern Virginia, November 1999

"Good evening, sir, welcome to the Inn of the Valley. Did you have a reservation?" The host was formally dressed, blond with dark streaks in his short hair, infuriatingly young, and he struck Dr. Roger Gardner as being almost aggressively gay.

"I didn't have a reservation, I was tossed out of a speeding car on the highway, and this is the first place I could walk to," Dr. Gardner managed to say through swollen lips.

"Oh . . . kay. Let me see what we can do. It is a ninety-five-dollar prix fixe dinner, you know . . ." The host looked expectantly at Dr. Gardner to see whether this information would scare him away.

"I didn't want to eat. I wanted to call my . . . girl, my wi . . . my —"

"Life partner?" the host offered helpfully.

"Yes, to tell her I'm okay, and that maybe she should send a cab down to pick me up."

"We can arrange a taxi for you, sir," the host said in the fond hope that the stranger in the messed-up black suit with what looked like bloodstained feathers mashed into it might take the hint, and the cab, and leave the meticulously overdecorated lobby before any more debris spilled off him.

"That would mark the end of a perfect day," Dr. Gardner said.

30
FILAQUONSETT
RESERVATION
JANUARY 2000

To: BabyCasey@aol.com
From: Dideeman@hotmail.com
Subject: ixnay

Yes, I owe my brother in the BBU a modicum of loyalty, but no self-respecting Big Baby with an ounce of authority should even consider holding another event in or near the Filaquonsett (sic) Casino. Aside from the spurious nature of the tribe (sic)'s origins, this place is hotter than a nuclear waste dump. Word: It could be dangerous to do business with these people.

Casey looked at the message on the BBU chat board, stared at it for five, then ten, minutes while his blood, and his pants, ran cold. Who was "Dideeman"? How did he find Casey in the most secure bulletin-board environment on the Internet? What did he mean the Big F was dangerous?

Barbara Menzies was close to her break. In her regulation Filaqonsett buckskin shirt-jac and navy trousers, she was dealing for a table full of tourists from Dedham, Massachusetts, one of whom Barbara had already expelled from the table for card counting. To her, people who tried to "game" the game were parasites on the body of blackjack. Never one to shrink from a confrontation (she had once famously called a former first lady touring the former Gammage "a lesbian trapped inside a man's body"), Barbara saw the first sign of a "system" as her signal to politely but firmly ask the player to leave the table. This one happened to be a personal-injury lawyer, and he mumbled something about suing. She responded, in a voice loud enough for the high rollers in the enclosed baccarat lounge to hear, "Sir, last time I checked, you cannot sue a sovereign nation. Good night." All she left out was, "Try the veal, putz."

Half an hour later, after the Dedhamites, duly abashed, had turned over their last dollar to the tribe, Casey took her elbow and hustled her into The Roasting Beaver. Not even pausing to order, they sat at one of the little burled oak tables, staring at the keno board above the cashier until Barbara said, "I'm on a fifteen, what's the deal?" Casey looked over his shoulder like a salesman preparing to tell a racist joke, then took a deep breath. Barbara was afraid he was preparing to ask her about the Tribal Council's hottest rumor, that she'd been the sole guest at one of Daria Long's schnitzel dinners, but Casey was vaguer, and grimmer. "I can't tell you how, but I think we're being threatened by somebody."

"Who's we, Tonto?" Barbara smirked with a notable lack of amusement. "Look, Casey, we know the Wowosas don't like us, we know the State wants to shake us down, but, all due respect to Mr. Tony Silotta, the man's a paranoid creep." She paused to look up at the ceiling and, relieved to see no viewing panels above her, continued. "Get real. Everybody's got enemies, and any Indian tribe that's sitting on a gold mine has got to have some white-eyes gunning for it. That may be why we've got half the town working as security. Now, I got tourists to fleece, okay?"

31
WASHINGTON, D.C.
FEBRUARY 2000

"In this part of the operation," Lieutenant General Lucius Clay Adams intoned, "the contaminated soil is superheated to a temperature where the silica is melted to glass. As the radioactive substance cools, it becomes, in effect, an obsidian prison for the isotopes, allowing them to do their half-life thing in relative peace and quiet. Now, of course," the Army Corps of Engineers chief added, "I'm no nuclear physicist, but that's the way our boys tell me it works and, in terms of reliability, they say it's equal or superior to any of our hydroelectric dam projects. And that's *dam* good." He couldn't help himself. He'd always been known, since his days in UCLA ROTC, to be blessed with an irrepressible, if not world-class wit, and here, with two high-ranking chieftains of a major East Coast Indian tribe attending a private briefing on the rather serious subject of nuclear waste disposal, he was indulging his love of tiresome wordplay.

Then, brushing his leathery right hand through short-cropped red hair, General Adams got serious again. "The people in Nevada are pretty upset about the current plan to bury this stuff out there, so the interest you gentlemen are showing, I'd say, is more than welcome right about now. Obviously, I've been tasked to take the temperature of a lot of tribal organizations, and, to be brutally honest about it, you two are the first to actually come in and see the facts for yourselves. It's not so scary, once you understand the science, is it?"

Joseph Catspaw and Don Nightswim traded glances. There was concern, almost discomfort, in their looks. They were sitting just across a small, rectangular table from General Adams, in the Corps of Engineers' seldom-used small conference room. And, as it happened, the general had an acid reflux problem that gave his breath, this particular morning, the odor of a California brush fire, all creosote and rodent-corpse. Stifling his discomfort, Joseph turned back to the ruddy man in the uniform. "Well, you know, as a tribal leader, I'm responsible to my ancestors and my . . . my post-ancestors to not poison our Mother." Don

225

nodded solemnly.

"Nobody's going to be poisoning any-body's mother around here," General Adams said in his most reassuring tone. "We can build a repository designed and engineered to withstand six nuclear winters. And, God's honest truth, or whatever deity you happen to worship, what we'd put up would be a lot more impervious to the elements than what they have out in Yucca Mountain. Tell you something, Chief, and —"

"Assistant chief," Don offered.

"— The people in Nevada can enjoy the luxury of worrying about something that might happen ten thousand years from now. But, for a tribe like yours, this could be a life-saver. You know, the Havasupai Navajos have been able to start two new schools and a full-sized Circle K since they accepted a low-level waste depot on their land."

"How many schools did they have before?" Joseph felt an urge to keep the conversation going, though he was bullshitting the bullshitter just fine. Sometimes, he just needed to prolong the challenge.

"I don't actually have anything on that," General Adams conceded. "The people at the Energy Department didn't put that in my briefing book."

"In fact, though" — Joseph knew he had the guy, the sale was closed, the consignment of jeans was leaving the warehouse, the invoices were already printed up, but he needed to put up one more simulacrum of resistance — "this isn't low-level waste you're talking about for our location, it's high-level waste, right? And this would be directly adjacent to our casino. I mean, I don't know, I may be one dumb Indian, but doesn't that pose a much greater danger to . . ."

"To Mother," Don finished.

"To Mother," Joseph whispered.

Lieutenant General Lucius Clay Adams said to himself, I need this like I need a second anus. I offer to help get some people at Energy out of a political jam, I troll for some redskins needy enough to put a ticking A-bomb on their property in exchange for a few pieces of wampum, and all I get in response is this cigar-store Indian who's probably never been out of the Bronx, and his pal the Braidman of Alcatraz, and now they're giving me grief about gamma rays and roentgens."

While engrossed in his inner monologue, the general fumbled around for the remote control that could operate the slide show on his laptop. The computer was actually close enough that he could tap the keyboard to cue the visuals, but the remote gave him a keener sense of command.

"Let me show you something," he announced as the presentation's splash screen glowed its welcome. "This," the first bar on a chart, "shows the amount of radiation exposure Americans get annually from X-rays and other medical procedures. This" — and a second bar popped on accompanied by the sound of a chime — "is the amount of radiation exposure Americans get annually from airport and building security apparatus."

"Wow," Don enthused.

"Yes. Wow, indeed. And this —"

As the third bar popped on-screen, to the sound of a higher chime, Joseph began gathering his papers and signaled to Don to present to General Adams a piece of something that looked like dirty parchment. "This is an agreement written on the skin of the year's first elk. It is our most official document. On behalf of our brothers and sisters of the Filaquonsett Nation, we accept your offer to let us host a nuclear waste facility on our reservation, and agree to all terms, however punitive. May the sun god shine upon you. May the rain god shower you with fertility. May the —"

"You sure you don't want to see the third bar?" General Adams asked Joseph.

"You know what? I'll skip the third god, you'll put the third bar on hold. Sorry, but I got a three o'clock with a guy in Bethesda who says he's got a complete set of *Charles in Charge* characters." And Joseph signaled to Don that they had used enough of the great white man's time.

Five minutes later, as he sipped a celebratory Stoli and water, General Adams mused, Yes. Wow, indeed. Awfully easy pickings. That chief must be one shitty poker player. In the hallway, taking the long walk back toward the building's highly secured exit, Joseph Catspaw low-fived Don Nightswim.

32
FILAQUONSETT RESERVATION
MARCH 2000

"Ladies and gentlemen, the management of the Filaquonsett Casino welcomes you, and reminds you that at no time during the show should flash photography be used, as it may panic the snow leopards. And now, first up, please welcome, the Elvis of Bangkok, Sugat Thanakorn!"

"I thought this place used to have big-name entertainment, what the —"

Tony Silotta put a firm hand on the forearm of Vince Winstanley. "The price of front-row comps is you don't knock the talent," he hissed through his new mustache. Then he flashed the $10,000 Silotta grin at Eileen, and, with a flourish, poured some more Dom in each of their glasses while Sugat Thanakorn began a rousing rendition of what sounded like "Fats Alightmonmon."

"By the way, Eileen, the Warhols really jazz up the fashion arcade. I never knew he painted Geronimo and those guys."

"He didn't," Eileen Winstanley said while sipping her Dom. "But Studio Warholia does. By the hundreds. All the NatAm casinos are buying them. Not," she added proudly, "at the price we got them for."

"Tony," Vince persisted, "what's the deal? How come you're buying imitation any-things all of a sudden?"

Tony Silotta closed down his smile for the season, and suddenly Vince began to understand the price of pushing the man faster than he wanted to go. It was only after the plaintive strains of "Ruffmeat Endo" started up that Tony deigned to respond.

"Listen, Vince, suddenly you got some real lobbying to do for us."

"Legislative advocacy," Vince corrected, until Tony's steel-eyed look shut him up good.

"Somehow some fuckhead at the Corps of Engineers is convinced that this is the best place on God's green earth to store radioactive crap until it stops glowing."

"You're kidding," Vince whispered as the crowd applauded respectfully.

"If Reeny wasn't having surgery, she'd tell you, Tony Silotta only kids on April Fools' Day."

Eileen spoke out of curiosity and concern. "Anything serious — I mean the surgery?"

"Nah, she's just getting her nipples made permanently erect." He turned back to Vince as Eileen reflexively shuddered. "There's got to be some committee or some governor's something that can stop this before it turns our little gold mine into a fucking depleted uranium mine. You gotta find the off button on this deal and hammer it with extreme prejudice. And, for your information, the reason that the civilians are being treated to fake Warhols and Asian Elvises is that you're gonna have a nice little war chest to help you with your persuading." Tony grinned, and Vince felt as if he'd just become a great white shark's best friend.

33

FILAQUONSETT
RESERVATION
APRIL 2000

Earlene Hammond was honking like a Canada goose with scrambled migration radar. Her BBC accent was flowing, through some unaccountable vocal plumbing that had become her on-air trademark, straight through her nose, and then into the business end of a top-of-the-line Beymann 820U microphone. She had learned to modulate, to moderate the squawk during the recent good times — she had even taken the Filaquonsett name Silent Fox — but the thrust of her peroration this morning was that the gravy train might soon be running out of track.

"Tribesmembers have been most generous in the last year, and as a result, we've been able, for the first time since we went on the air, we've been able to bring you all of *Morning Edition* throughout our pledge drives with just the briefest of interruptions. But we are now facing what may be our most severe challenge in the history of this radio station." In the next studio, converted for the occasion into a war room, volunteers manned computers and phone banks, and an LCD plasma screen hung on the wall indicated the number of callers per hour, the number of new and returning subscribers per hour, and the current running total of pledges. Silent Fox's tone of barely controlled paranoia was designed not just to scare the listeners, but to force the volunteers' adrenaline level to overwhelm their fatigue. True to her training in the front lines of public radio, she was administering aural epinephrine.

"If the Filaquonsett reservation becomes the site of the world's largest nuclear waste storage facility, I can promise you this: We will have no more live music on Saturday nights, we will have no more BBC World Service in the early mornings, we will probably not even be able to afford to create new programs in the wonderful *Filaquonsett Way* series, which has brought so many of us so much closer to our roots. Because we have to have the funds to continue broadcasting while we're helping to oppose this bizarre and dangerous scheme to destroy our community, you have to not only renew your pledge — you have to increase it. Otherwise — excuse me, somebody in Master Control, what's that buzzing in my headphones?"

Reeny Silotta was on the biggest mission of her life. Not that her life consisted of that many missions, but this was a big one. She had had surgery, all right, but nipple erection was just — as Tony had put it, with an almost blindingly accurate accidental simile — "the maraschino cherries on the sundae." The real agenda of the afternoon in Dr. Hockter's office was to adjust Serena's already-perfect facial features subtly enough that she could escape recognition during the next forty-eight hours. After that, Tony assured her, and the doctor agreed, if she wanted to return to her current look, she could.

"My face is my face, Tony, I've looked this way for almost two years now, how could I —"

And then Tony put a finger to his lips, glared at her fixedly, and the appointment was made.

A week later, the bandages off and the swelling down, Serena Silotta put on the most demure, non-attention-getting outfit in her closet, a slinky black dress with spaghetti straps, kissed Tony good-bye, and headed across the George Washington Bridge to deliver a package to somebody she didn't know.

"Why," she had asked Tony in a moment when she thought he might be in the mood for something as nervy as a question from his fuckin' wife, "why can't you send one of your guys to do this little delivery? I'm a covered dancer, not a mule."

Tony had been reading the luxury-property ads in *The Wall Street Journal,* so he was in an unusually good mood. He put the paper down and motioned Serena over to him. Then he gave her a very sharp slap on the ass. "Reeny, my 'guys,' as you call them, blend in about as well as a cockroach on a wedding cake."

"Hell, I don't exactly look like Marge from bookkeeping. Besides, you always say you don't want me involved in your work."

"Sweetie," Tony said as he picked up the *Journal* and gazed longingly at a three-acre property in Umbria, asking price $47 million, "just take the fuckin' package and get your ass out of this town house before I tear off your new nipples and flush them down the crapper."

Now she was heading up the Sawmill River Parkway, checking the directions Tony had had printed out for her. They consisted of a name, a Mr. Nightswim, and an address. As she turned off at the designated Exit 203, she realized it was the address of the Wowosa Casino.

Don Nightswim's office at Wowosa was a symphony of redwood. Redwood paneling, redwood shelves, a burled redwood desk, redwood mini-blinds (actually plastic, but the look was the same) — it all served to remind Don, every minute he was in his office and his eyes were open (for, in truth, he was a regular napper), that life had gotten seriously better. Joe Katz had met him at a clothing retailers' convention, to which Payless had sent Don Nyswang as a perk for selling more than his quota of that season's $100 women's running sneakers, and when tribalism reared its lovely head in Connecticut, Joe had remembered the moon-faced guy with the light cocoa skin and the distant eyes and offered him "a major role in the tribe."

Don's role, more often than not, was to insulate Joseph Catspaw from bad news. When Bally wanted to charge more for their

Indian-themed slots, Don dealt with it. When zoning officials of the neighboring county objected to Wowosa building a ten-story parking structure, Don dealt with it. And now today, with this strangely attractive woman walking in this very sexy way into his office, Don was determined to deal with it.

"Hello, Miss . . ."

"Just call me . . ." Serena realized she'd just been expecting to drop the package off at some flunky's desk, and she hadn't spent a moment of time in the car thinking about her alias. She searched her Vegas memory bank and finally came up with it. "Just call me Elvisa."

"All right, then. Interesting name."

"My parents were big Elvis fans. My dad thinks he's alive, and my mom thinks he's God." Serena was now happily riffing, the kind of thing she used to do in the dressing room with her fellow covered dancers.

"Well, if he's alive, we'd certainly like to talk to him about appearing in our showroom," Don enthused. "Speaking of which, you look like you have a little showroom in you."

"I —" and Serena felt a twinge not in her new nipples, which were bereft of nerve endings, but in her mind, recalling Tony's threat to the new buds. She snapped out of conversation mode with whiplash speed. "I have a package for you. Really, that's all I have to say." She handed a brown-paper-wrapped box across the paperless redwood desk to Don and stood to leave.

"Gee, we were just getting to know each other. Would you like a bottle of Wowosa Water for the road? We're bottling our own springy water now, we can't use the word 'spring,' it's actually just tap water that we run through a two-bit mineralizer, but it tastes pretty damn —"

Before he could finish his encomium to local hydrogen dioxide, Serena had opened the large redwood door and slinkily sashayed out of Don's life. He pressed his remote door-closer and sat down to examine the package. The first thing he noticed was a printed note: "To be opened only by Joseph Catspaw."

Twenty minutes later, Joseph Catspaw was shaking, quivering, and sweating with a fear he hadn't known since the two Israeli brothers had threatened to run him through his own stone-washing machinery and sell his skin as a pair of stylishly distressed jeans. Don Nightswim had brought in the package, told Joseph about the showgirl-type woman who'd delivered it, and then left to deal with a little musicians' union problem in the showroom.

Joseph was intrigued by the package. He picked it up, smelled it, shook it, then, relieved that it didn't appear to contain anything threatening, opened it. That's when the tremors of trepidation set in for real. There in the box was a pretty fair miniature replica of the bed in Joseph and Cheryl's master bedroom — same duvet and pillows, same carved eagle headboard. Some very fine miniature work, he noted to himself, but who . . . ? Now Joseph saw a shape under the little covers, and pulled them off. Lying there, right next to where he would be in the actual bed, was something he'd long heard about in the collectible underground but never been able to find: a miniature Chrissy from *Three's Company,* in absolutely mint condition, except for the fact that her head had been ripped off and lay on the far little pillow, her tiny blond ponytails floating in a pool of what looked remarkably like blood.

Johnny Pantoleone, head of the musicians' union local that represented tooters (as the trade magazine *Variety* called them) at all venues, Indian or regular, north of New York City and west of Boston, was shaking his head. Sitting at a table in the Wowosa showroom while sound engineers tried to isolate a pesky feedback problem, he was communicating to Don Nightswim the impossibility of his members' continuing to perform at their usual high level of proficiency with only fifteen-minute breaks between sets. Don was about to respond with what Johnny expected to be a hard-assed management line when the dark-skinned Indian's brown eyes blazed open, he stood up as if his chair were on fire, and he left their little confab as urgently as if he were being pursued by a swarm of particularly ill-tempered killer bees. What summoned him to the far-left showroom entrance was nothing more, or less, than the sulfurous gaze of Joe Catspaw.

"Who the fuck was she? Where the fuck was she from?" Joe demanded, while the PA system whistled a thousand-hertz tune.

"Who the fuck knows? I told you, all I clocked was that she had one hell of a body, topped off by the tits that O.J. was going to get for Nicole and her sisters before he had his little —"

Joseph was in no mood for trial-of-the-century nostalgia. "Listen, my friend. We've got these phony-baloney Indians on the run, but Tony Silotta plays rough. Never more so than when he finds himself holding a losing hand. Maybe you can't take the pressure. Maybe you're even doing a little *'cute'* with our friends up north."

Don Nightswim had dealt with Joe's temper before. Three years earlier, Wowosa's Washington lobbyist, Nate Yoblakoff, had charged the tribe three million dollars for "professional services," ostensibly for making friends with the incoming administration. A free Washington weekly had unearthed memos ("This gun doesn't just smoke, it inhales!" the headline blared) indicating the bulk of the money found its way to a riding academy attended by Yoblakoff's four daughters. When the news broke, Catspaw had gone more incandescent than the Vegas Strip on New Year's Eve, thundering to Cheryl at an Elton John rehearsal that the Yoblakoff daughters would find their horses a bit harder to control with their heads relocated to another state.

"The daughters?" Cheryl asked, shocked that her husband was sitting in a showroom entertaining the idea of multiple murder.

"The horses," Joe muttered.

At that point, Don Nightswim hopped the

Wowosa jet to a closed-door NNAGA session at the Piute Four Seasons Resort to suggest in no uncertain terms that there were far better ways to flush tribal resources down the white man's toilet. Before Nate Yablokoff could say "money laundry," his contracts had been cancelled by the Choctaws, Chippewas, Chickasaws, and a dozen other tribes, and the Yablokoff daughters were reduced to riding ponies at the Georgetown farmers' market.

But never before had Joseph's anger fixed Don squarely in its sights. The experience had Nightswim momentarily thinking that the four-bedroom Colonial manse on two acres of wooded property, the Cadillac Escalade, the ability to comp and be comped in any tribal enclave known to man, and all the other little perks of modern Native American life weren't worth the aggravation, the humiliation, the need to defend one's honesty and honor that was so flooding his nervous system with embarrassment. Don felt his cocoa complexion turning — of all things — momentarily red.

"Listen, Joe, if at any time you think I'm gaming the polygraph tests and you want to de-accession me, man, I'm at your mercy, you know that. I'll go back to Payless or I'll go across the street to Target. I got along before Wowosa, I can get along after Wowosa."

"That's exactly what worries me. No, my friend, now more than ever I gotta keep you close to me. Next thing I know, you'll go into the women's fashion-jeans business and a couple of Lebanese guys will decide that violates my old do-not-compete clause. Here — Joseph dipped into his alligator-skin wallet and fished out twelve C-notes — "buy a *'nice'* for your next girlfriend."

34
IRVINGTON,
NEW YORK
MAY 2000

Daria Long couldn't believe it. In the few months that Lucy Striker had lived in Irvington, she had managed to make her new apartment look absolutely as cluttered and unkempt, as full of yellowed newspapers and commission reports stuffed inside colored translucent plastic folders, as her old place back home. Daria had only seen Lucy's original abode, on the second floor of a stately old Victorian on Broken Arrow Way (formerly Second Street), once, when Daria was visiting everyone in town whom she might recruit to the ranks of Native American Sculpture Park supporters. Lucy was last on her list, and it wasn't that Daria so coveted the woman's support, she just sought to keep the indefatigable speaker at meetings from being a committed opponent. Lucy had shrugged at the time and just muttered something about "if it's so damned important to the whole Indian thing, why doesn't the casino pay for it?" and then offered Daria a cup of something tepid and murky that Lucy called tea.

Now Daria smoothed her peasant skirt on Lucy's IKEA sofa (even Lucy knew it was ugly, but she bought it because she liked its name: Knupe). Daria patiently explained to Lucy, with just a hint of incipient panic in her delivery, that the proposed nuclear waste storage facility would affect not only the Filaquonsett Reservation ("I knew this whole thing would end up even sadder than that stupid plan for tertiary sewage treatment," Lucy muttered in her dyspeptic monotone), but the entire area, even Irvington.

"The only way I can see it affecting us is that our sheriffs can start writing more speeding tickets once the casino business goes bust," Lucy said with a dark satisfaction.

"Darling, you still deal at the casino, don't you?"

"I'm on borrowed time there, anyway. Word on the floor is, they're replacing half the poker tables with machines. The darn machines are taking over the whole casino business, and they don't give the customer anywhere near as close to a decent break as a human dealer does. But the guys upstairs don't care about that, all they care about is that machines don't need rest breaks, machines don't need days off or sick leave or family leave or summer vacations or Christmas bonuses or —"

Daria felt a need to get back to the subject almost as strong as her need for oxygen. "It's going to leak into the water, it's going to leak into the air, these people are from the Corps of Engineers, they can't build something to last a hundred years, let alone ten thousand."

"You didn't seem to mind them when they built your beloved NASP. Heck, before I left the 'reservation' I collected at least a dozen news stories about wild birds trying to land there and getting snared in the 'art.' " Lucy didn't make air quotes, but her normal melancholy drone became exaggeratedly drawn out on the words in question, suggesting even deeper pools of sadness.

"Lucy, I know you. You came to my house, you ate my goulash. Of course we've had our disagreements, but I know that in your heart of hearts you're really not in favor of a nuclear waste dump anywhere near where you or I or anybody else lives." She waited for a response, but Lucy just dropped her head in what Daria regarded as silent acquiescence. Silence from Lucy was like a gift, and Daria wasn't about to return it unused.

"We're putting together a caravan of the nations, Indians and palefaces alike, to go over to Albany and testify before the State Environmental Control Commission. If they deny the permit, the thing doesn't get built, and you can continue to pester the people here about — what are your issues here?"

"Don't even start. These people have been over-fluoridating the water for years, they're exceeding all the known dosage limits, they know they're doing it, they're wasting our money on the fluoride, not to mention the damage to —"

"Okay, and I can go back to finding out why Donald Albuquerque hasn't finished his sculpture, *The First Condor,* which we desperately need for the centerpiece of the former bird sanctuary. My point is, my dear, first things first. Should I put this in the dishwasher?" Daria was standing now, holding the cup as tentatively as if it contained an equine urine sample.

"I don't have one. Just dump it in the sink on top of everything else."

■ ■ ■ ■

Filaquonsett Reservation, May 2000
"This is an odd time to be seeking recognition as a one-thirty-second Filaquonsett," Dr. Roger Gardner observed tightly. He was sitting in his ergonomically excellent leather armchair and just swiveled back slightly from his elegantly carved desk in his office at tribal headquarters, the one-time Sears store on Laughing Beaver Square. His gaze alternated between a marvelously forged affidavit of Filaquonsett origins, with citations dating back to the time of the Massachusetts Bay Colony, and the dark-skinned man with one braid who had proffered it for his consideration.

"Hey," the man said, "I'm an odd guy. I found myself in the wrong tribe, I did a little research, discovered my true origins, and at that point it was clear that I had to come home, give all I can to my real community. Including" — and here his voice lowered to a silky whisper that Dr. Gardner could barely hear above the roar of the tourist buses outside — "everything I know." What Don Nightswim knew, among other things, was that when you've already been virtually convicted of doing something, you might as well have the satisfaction of actually doing it. He also knew who in this neck of the woods had Samoans on the payroll.

35
ALBANY, NEW YORK
JUNE 2000

Vince Winstanley was just wrapping up the last of his sotto voce, ex parte conversations with two of the three members of the New York State Environmental Control Commission regarding the possibility of funding for their possible future runs for possible higher office, when the gavel sounded. The commission's chairman, seventy-three-year old Edgar Lamont, was calling to order a hearing on the planned and contracted-for siting of a nuclear waste disposal facility at the Filaquonsett Reservation. For somebody used to the ornate hearing rooms of official Washington — the fine marble, the rich woods, the high ceilings with the long reverberations that let incautiously delivered testimony hang in the air like rotting hams — this was more like the place where you came to get your taxes done. As Vince returned to his seat, disdainfully registering the low false-ceiling hiding harsh fluorescent

251

bulbs, the cheap wallboard, the assemble-it-yourself conference table, a familiar voice whispered in his right ear: "Having the last word before the hearing starts is an old trick, my friend, but it won't play today."

Hap Matthews was in the chair next to Vince. They were both among those invited to testify to the three commissioners, who sat around one end of the long table. Also testifying were Lieutenant General Lucius Clay Adams of the Army Corps of Engineers, a representative of the Nuclear Regulatory Commission in Washington whose nameplate identified him as Dr. Rupert Hellman, Director of Interagency Relations, and a young woman whom Vince was sure he recognized. Her long black hair was in braids, Indian-style, but she was wearing a stylish Ann Taylor suit. There was no nameplate in front of her.

Outside the hearing room, in the long corridor leading from the elevator landing, Daria, Lucy, Earlene, and their hardy band of supporters chanted "Waste not, store not" and other less-catchy slogans opposing the plan to put high-level nuclear waste on a parcel of land the tribe had reserved for casino expansion. Outside the building, on the lawn, stood twice as many protestors (their number dictated their location), chanting into the open window of the hearing room, "Don't break another treaty."

Inside, the testimony around the table was predictable: Vince vehemently challenged the authenticity of the agreement, Lieutenant General Clay said the Corps of Engineers had cleaned up its act, Hap said Indian tribes needed sources of income more reliable than the fickle finger of gaming (a phrase he was proud of; it came from seeing an infomercial for a DVD of old *Laugh-In* sketches on the hotel TV the night before), and Dr. Rupert Hellman affirmed that this facility was engineered to the same level of safety his agency had already approved for Yucca Mountain in Nevada, before the unpleasantness. There was nothing left on the agenda but to hear from the young lady in the suit.

"Distinguished Commissioners, fellow witnesses, my name is Jennifer New Moon, and I'm a vice chairman of the Native American Civil Rights Mobilization."

Chairman Lamont cleared his throat for what seemed like half an hour — an oratorio of phlegm removal — then leaned forward into his microphone: "You're a little young to be vice chairman of anything, aren't you, miss?"

As the other commissioners chuckled, more out of embarrassment (or fear of the feminist tirade that they were sure would follow) than amusement, Jennifer's brown eyes glared at him with a cold fire. Lamont shrugged the shoulders of his gray suit, which at this point in his life were several inches broader than his own shoulders, and slumped back to his listening position.

"She on your side again?" Hap whispered to Vince, launching the temporary conversational conspiracy of opponents, like Civil War combatants exchanging pleasantries after dark. "I had no idea she was coming," Vince whispered back. Hap raised his eyebrows in mild disbelief, the way he did when Vince first told him he didn't drink. "So, *entre nous*, whose stooge might she be?" Hap wondered in an almost-too-loud whisper.

Jennifer continued as if Edgar Lamont's interruption had been a shared hallucination in the minds of her audience. "More than two hundred years. More than one hundred forty-seven treaties. A consistent record. All of them signed. And all of them broken. Today we see another treaty between the 'Great White Father' " — and her air quotes dripped with sarcasm so heavy they could sink a blimp — "and a legally constituted tribe of Native Americans. Maybe I wouldn't sign this treaty. Maybe *Mr. Winstanley* wouldn't. But it is long past time for the white man to decide what's legitimate and what's not legitimate for tribal officials to do. The sovereign nation of the Filaquonsetts, for good and sufficient reasons of their own, believe a nuclear waste storage facility engineered to the proper level of safety and security will be a positive contribution to their community. If there is no environmental reason why this pact should not be honored, please don't step in the foul footprints of your forefathers and dash yet another tribal treaty against the rocks of racism."

Vince knew better than to blurt from the audience during someone else's testimony, but he couldn't help himself. "But those aren't the signatures of —"

A gaveling from the chairman was evidence enough that, on this particular day, in this particular chamber, the heartfelt voice of three centuries of genocide and betrayal would not be ignored.

"I guess," Vince said to Hap as he gathered up his papers and stuffed them into his briefcase, "she was your stooge."

Hap smiled a rictus of modest triumph.

"As they say in the casinos, some days you just get lucky. *C'est la vie, mon frere.*"

■ ■ ■ ■

PART THREE

■ ■ ■ ■

36
FILAQUONSETT
RESERVATION
NEW YORK, JUNE
2000

Dick Stillwater was driving his Jag XKE along the Boulevard of the Fathers, the former Main Street, daring the late afternoon breeze to ruffle his hair, when his cell phone tinkled "The Flight of the Bumblebee." When he clicked on, something even more frantic was at the other end.

"Dick? It's over. *Finis.* Time to get out, time to move on, time to get your spurs a jingle-jangle-jingling. *Capeesh?*" Dr. Roger Gardner sounded as if all his hard-won poise and savoir faire had been sucked down some cosmic drain, leaving him with a handful of multilingual clichés and a dark despair. He sounded, though Dick didn't dare visualize the thought, as if he'd even taken his vest completely off. Dick, swerving to avoid a tourist bus hurtling toward him, taking the sheep to their tribal fleecing, wanted to pull over and give the man a hug. Not a literal hug, mind you — Dick was deeply engrossed in a stormy affair with a reheaded pit boss — but a warm bath of verbal sympathy was what Dick had in mind.

"Listen, my friend," he lullabyed into his handset, "nothing's wrong that a hot week-end with some tight slots won't fix. The reservations for *Redfeet!: A Native American Riverdance* are going through the roof, the zoning caucus is totally wired to approve the additional tower for the hotel, what could possibly —" Dick caught a glimpse of himself in the rear view mirror as Dr. Roger Gardner gave him the news from Albany. The piece looked good. The silver and gray intermixed with the few remaining strands of my own hair, Dick thought, is an utterly convincing —

"They what? You've got to be kidding. This is asinine. I don't care if we have the slots set to guaranteed one hundred percent payoff, no one will want to spend one frigging nanosecond in a radius of one hundred fifty miles of this place. You're kidding, Roger, I know you, and I appreciate the hell out of the joke, but —"

"Dick, I'm not kidding. The party's over. It's time to call it a day. They've done whatever the hell they did to our pretty balloons. The piper must be paid."

Dick realized to his horror that the worst had actually happened. The man he most looked up to in the entire world, the man he knew to be the smartest human in New York State north of the Bronx, Dr. Roger Gardner, was drunk.

The messages were piling up on Chief Zorn's voice mail: calls from attorneys representing the luxury stores in the retail arcade, all invoking — as if they'd agreed on it at a breakfast strategy meeting at the Waldorf's Peacock Alley, as, in fact, they had — the force majeure clause of their contracts. Unusually for such clauses, these included the possibility of a nuclear-waste dump being sited within a twenty-mile radius of the arcade. Curtis thought glumly, as he tapped through the messages, Somebody's lawyer just earned himself a big bonus.

In his e-mail in-box were cancellation notices from Celine Dion, who suddenly decided that a previously undiagnosed illness would make it impossible for her to fulfill her agreement to appear at Club Suit for the agreed-upon six weeks per annum over the next seven years, and Jerry Seinfeld, whose representative explained that the stress of running his own advertising agency was taking a greater toll than Mr. Seinfeld had anticipated. The final message was from Mike Schwarzwelder of Wal-Mart. It said, simply, "Ignore previous message."

"We are *live* from the emergency special session of the Council of Elders and, because of this live broadcast, *Marketplace* will not be heard tonight." Behind Earlene Hammond's voice, the sound of barely controlled uproar, as people who hadn't been to a Council of Elders meeting since Recognition Day clamored for the few available seats. Chief Zorn was attempting to be heard over the ruckus, banging the buffalo head to no avail.

"Please, fellow tribesmembers, don't make me use the gavel. It's not the Filaquonsett Way." The hubbub crescendoed, the crowd oblivious. "Oh, what the hell."

And Earlene, who was herself still adrift in the sea of her own disbelief at the turn of civic events, signaled furiously to her engineer to put her on the air again, to explain that which needed no explanation.

"Chief Curtis Zorn is gaveling the Council of Elders into some kind of order. And let me just say" — and here her voice became Earlene's impression of a sportscaster at a golf match as the room finally began to quiet down — "that whatever happened in Albany and whatever happens here tonight, we still need you to fulfill your pledges. If you specified the WQUO headdress when you made your pledge, your-check-must-be-received-by-midnight-Friday." She sped up remarkably to get the last sentence in before the chief began speaking.

"Okay, I'm going to move that we dispense with the staff report," Chief Curtis Zorn said with brisk dispatch, "since we all know —"

"Second." Barbara Menzies, doing her hand exercises even though she knew her best dealing days might be behind her, was first to the mike. "Let's cut to the goddamn chase. What do we do now?" The crowd roared its approval of the question, hoping against hope that one of the tribe's elders (though they were younger than many in the room) had a clue about an answer.

"We could take an expedited appeal to the federal courts, try to get to the Supreme Court before this term is up," Casey Elliott offered.

Barbara Menzies shot Casey a stern look. "They aren't eager to take on challenges to

263

Native American sovereignty. To put it very mildly."

"But this was a forgery. Nobody in authority in this tribe signed those documents," Casey whined.

"We all know that," Chief Zorn admonished, "but once the federal government starts looking behind the surface of tribal agreements, all hell breaks loose with hundreds of tribes in all fifty states and, frankly, that's just a can of worms nobody wants to eat."

Casey couldn't help himself. "Well, is there a can of worms that anybody does want to eat . . . from?"

Barbara Menzies looked at him as if he were an infant. Casey's face reddened, and his diaper filled.

On Central Park West in New York City at that exact moment, Tony Silotta was decking *David,* punching the two-fifths-sized replica of the classic statue with a roundhouse right that immediately began to hurt like hell. Which didn't improve his mood one bit.

"Those fucking goombahs," Tony howled at Serena, who was sitting quietly at the dining room table, her face still slightly swollen from her recent surgical rewind, picking at four arugula leaves in a walnut-oil dressing. "This is their revenge for Tony Silotta going out on his own. They couldn't stand it that I had a fucking sense of style, that I put a goddamn art museum in a town that thought a museum was a place where you displayed Liberace's old rubbers. They couldn't stand it that I went to actual banks and got actual loans instead of just raiding the pension fund of some fucking bullshit union."

"Tone, honey, don't have a heart attack, sweetie," Reeny urged hopefully from the table as her husband, shirtless and heedless to possible infarctions or occlusions, continued to pace around the columns and pilasters and pediments of the living room like an aroused lion, one with a freshly injured paw, in a neoclassical zoo. "This is so *fucking unbelievable,*" Tony sputtered, slamming his left fist on an Indonesian teak occasional table. That made two gestures of anger, two hurt hands. "I've got a contract with the goddamn Circus des Artistes that stretches so far out into the future, one of the members of that suck-ass company might actually turn hetero. I've got Native American art commissions from that fucking Eileen

Winstanley coming out my goddamn crack. I've got —"

"Maybe people will still want to come, honey. Maybe we just have to make the slots looser," Serena offered hopefully as she took sparrow-sized bites of an arugula leaf without actually swallowing the thing.

"That's right, Reeny, everybody in their right mind will gladly run the risk of being radiated into a piece of fucking burnt and glowing cinnamon raisin toast for the sake of an extra chance or two to score a five-dollar jackpot on the fucking Ed McMahon slot machine. That's good thinking, baby. Eat some fucking leaves and please do me the favor to shut the fuck up."

This was serious. In all the time they'd been married, Tony had never before said "please" to her.

The Council of Elders meeting was in a total uproar, ancient Arnold Lipshitz yelling hoarsely over the crowd, "Civil disobedience, shut down the machine." Barbara Menzies wearily swung the gooseneck mike toward her, moaned, "Tribemember Lipshitz, we are all enormously upset, but the yelling of forty-year-old left-wing slogans, much as they might bring back pleasant memories, really isn't a lot of help to us

266

right now," and pushed the gooseneck away again. Casey picked disconsolately at the feathers in his headdress. Earlene, between reminders that a $1,000 patriarch pledge entitled you to free seats in the main casino showroom for five nights next year, lamented, "The Filaquonsett Way seems to be breaking down. We are all acting very Gammage tonight."

Anna Manybirds glided gracefully to the podium and was recognized to speak. The room quieted down. "The Filaquonsett tribe is facing a crisis," she said softly, her red-and-black blanket undulating softly as her arms beneath it waved to accentuate her words. "Some years ago, my tribe, the Tlingit, faced a terrible crisis. The elk were being shot, the salmon were being fished by the white man to the point of extinction, and the children were being exposed to an alien culture that soured them on their own traditions, their own ways. We had a solemn retreat and decided to borrow a ritual tradition from our Kwakiutl brothers in what you call Washington State. We held a potlatch. We gave away all our worldly possessions. We purified ourselves, and returned to the Spirit."

Daria Long, sitting cross-legged on the floor, found this more than even her broadmindedness could bear. With some effort, she stood up and almost shouted at the podium, "Pardon me, dear, but what did that accomplish, exactly?"

Chief Zorn tapped the buffalo head on the floor and admonished Daria for being out of order. Then he indicated to Anna that her time was almost up. Anna Manybirds looked straight at Daria. "Well," she said quietly and slowly, "it made it much easier for me to pack up and move here."

37
LAS VEGAS, NEVADA
FEBRUARY 2002

One year to the day after the Filaquonsett Reservation Nuclear Waste Disposal Facility became a done deal, the front page of the second section of the *Las Vegas Review Journal* ran a two-column headline: "Town's Latest Gem Opens Tonight: Strip Set to 'Go Native' with Nativia Resort," above a picture of a smiling Anthony J. Silotta standing in front of a resort casino that looked for all the world like a five-sixths-sized replica of the Big F. In fact, that's exactly what it was. The two giant carved hawks that had once adorned the front of the Filaquonsett now stood guard in the blazing Vegas sun, flanking an entryway that led into a cavernous entrance, past which statues of buffaloes by various Native American artists escorted you down a wide corridor on whose ceiling a light sculpture depicted abstracted images of Native American history in time to a recorded loop of Anasazi drumming. Past the coffee roaster was a casino that mimicked the Big F in every detail, down to the VIP slots room, the Elk Room for high rollers, and the Noble Elk Room for crazy high rollers from Malaysia.

But the Nativia, true to Vegas tradition, was more than just a replica (of what itself was a Native American copy of a Vegas casino). In a lounge adjoining the baccarat tables on the high-class end of the casino floor, Anna Manybirds had choreographed *Pow-Wow-Wow!,* a revue of Native American dances featuring girls recruited by Serena Silotta from her database of dancing nudes. Dealers were dressed in buckskin outfits and feathered headdresses, all the slots were Geronimos, the poker machines were custom-made "Beat Custer" models, and in the 1,000-seat Gray Wolf Theater, the Circus des Artistes had produced *Peace Pipe!,* a spectacular show of mime, water, and smoke effects depicting a revisionist interpretation of Wounded Knee in which the Native Americans emerged triumphant, if wet. Coming next was a vastly enlarged production of *Redfeet!*

On the casino floor, Barbara Menzies was,

if not the slickest blackjack dealer on the Strip, perhaps the happiest. She had made the acquaintance, on her first visit to downtown's Fremont Street, of a singer in a Spice Girls cover band who liked her women big and butch. They were now sharing the faux Posh's apartment just off West Sahara Boulevard, and Barbara was making discreet inquiries about a trip to Massachusetts for a certain ceremony.

Dick Stillwater had taken his act into the office of the hotel's director of Food and Beverage Services, where he once again negotiated with the Cokes and Pepsis of the world, along with the wineries, breweries, and, now most crucially for the new Vegas, the celebrity chefs of the world. His most recent success had been convincing Jamie Brown Bear, who had built a five-star restaurant specializing in elk and caribou dishes in a Menominee-operated casino-hotel in Michigan's Upper Peninsula, to open a branch in the Nativia in time for the grand opening. Dick celebrated by treating himself to a trip to Switzerland for a new, still-secret but highly regarded European surgical scalp procedure.

Dr. Roger Gardner had recovered nicely from his injuries and his flirtation with alcohol. Through Tony's good offices, he had resumed his educational career, now as head of the new Department of Native American Development at the University of Nevada-Las Vegas, where the nature of the doctorate that adorned his CV was not held against him.

Behind the hotel towers, Daria Long had transplanted the former Sculpture Park artworks to stand and cavort along the fairways and sandtraps and water hazards of a Robert Trent Jones Jr.-designed, eighteen-hole golf course. In the second-floor shopping arcade, Casey Elliott was managing The Squaw's Surprise, a 5,000-square-foot showcase of exotic sex toys and liquored-up chocolates.

Of the tribal elders, only Curtis Zorn had stayed in upstate New York, shedding his feathers and donning a suit to become chief public-relations representative for the waste-disposal facility, spending his days churning out reassuring press releases about canisters of radioactive glass being sealed in yard-thick containment vessels of steel-reinforced concrete inside advanced housings designed by the Corps of Engineers to survive for, at a minimum, ten thousand years. The facility itself was recruiting for workers among those least likely to object to the conditions and (according to Curtis) barely existent hazards of the jobs, residents of nearby, economically depressed counties who happened to be Native Americans whose tribes had not yet built casinos.

Vince and Eileen Winstanley had returned to Washington, relieved to be off the cutting edge of American gaming. Vince was guiltily convinced that he should have heeded the danger signs so apparent to Eileen on their first trip to Vegas. His wife's regrets were mixed with a reluctant nostalgia for life in the art world's fast lane. Working some civil service magic, Vince landed another GS-18 position at Interior, evaluating which species might still have a prayer of making it to the endangered list. Where lobbying was concerned, he told friends, he just happened to enter the world with the DNA to do the catching rather than the pitching. Eileen got more serious about showing their Great Danes, garnering a Best of Breed at the most recent Eukanuba show.

Lieutenant General Lucius Clay Adams was spending a lot of his time in Congress, explaining in meticulously vetted testimony the cost overruns and construction delays that were marring the opening of the disposal facility, keeping the containers of high-level wastes still sitting at the plants around the country that had generated them

273

and that were now entering their third decade of expecting to get rid of them.

Arnold Lipshitz had moved his belongings down State Route 28 to Irvington, now living in the same apartment building as Lucy Striker. They enjoyed the platonic pleasures of taking the bus to City Council meetings together, where they'd stay until the wee hours submitting chits and hectoring the representatives on subjects ranging from tardy garbage collections to unseemly arts grants.

Three and a half weeks after Nativia's grand opening, at which Wayne Newton sang both "The Star Spangled Banner" and the old hit "Indian Nation," Joseph Catspaw awoke to a beautiful spring morning, all blossoms and birdsong. Life was good again for the Wizard of Wowosa, as an Indian gaming trade magazine had dubbed him. Acceding to his wife Cheryl's repeated requests, he had hired a non-Arab contractor to supervise the renovations on the family house, and the Catspaws had just enjoyed a leak-free winter, the pots and pans relieved of living room duty. The reconstruction and the private-school tuition increases for Max and Sam ($30,000 a year each to teach sixth-grade kids how many states there are in the U.S.) were more than accommodated by Wowosa's suddenly increased slice of the region's Indian gaming pie, a fact celebrated by the voice of James Earl Jones in the resort's latest saturation ad campaign: "The only thing that's hot here is the action!"

But, shortly after his habitual breakfast (fresh-squeezed OJ, bagel with smoked buffalo, green tea), it dawned on Joseph that this just might be a day to remember. Entering the carport for the 7.4-mile commute to his office, Catspaw noticed something odd, interesting, even disturbing about his champagne-colored Mercedes SUV. Since he last saw it the previous evening, the luxury vehicle's hood had received a large dent, the approximate size and shape of a human body — as if, overnight, in the landscape between the windshield and the hood ornament, two people had done the wild thing. Odd, Joseph thought, because his days of going off the reservation for a little *'cute'* " were long gone — at least until the kids were in college.

At around 10:30 that morning, an hour after Don Nightswim had departed, with uncharacteristic enthusiasm, for a day trip to Elmira to track down a reported mint set of the original CHiPS, a package arrived on Joseph Catspaw's desk. This time it was brought not by a mysterious woman named Elvisa but in the more ordinary manner, via an overnight delivery service. The sender was indicated on the invoice as simply "A. Fan," with the return address that of the Wowosa Casino and the sender's phone number listed as Joseph's own private line.

Inside the package, sealed in an airtight plastic bag, was a beautifully woven blanket executing an intricate, abstract Navajo design in brilliant reds and oranges and sandy browns, a masterful example of the survival of Native American craftsmanship. It had the recognizable near-perfection of the best indigenous handiwork, punctuated only by the deliberate flaw the craftsman had inserted as a reminder of humanity's frailty. Joseph held the piece up to admire it, then he made a little show of displaying it for his cabinets full of miniature television stars of the past. "Look, boys and girls, somebody did a *'nice,'*" he advised them. Finally, he spread the blanket on his desk and ran his hands along its expanse, taking them for a stroll across its warmly nubby weave.

Only then did he notice a small Post-it note, which had been stuck to the Bubble Wrap surrounding the plastic envelope. The text of the note was printed in fourteen-point Helvetica Medium, the most generic of all computer-printer fonts. "To Mr. Joseph Katz," it began, already rubbing him the wrong way with his pre-Wowosa name. "Hope you got your smallpox shot."

ABOUT THE AUTHOR

Harry Shearer is familiar to millions as the voice of several characters on *The Simpsons.* He is a former writer and cast member on *Saturday Night Live,* and has appeared in numerous films including *This is Spinal Tap, A Mighty Wind,* and *For Your Consideration.* Harry's nationally syndicated radio show, *Le Show,* has been on the air for 16 years in most major markets, and his political blog runs on huffingtonpost.com. He lives in Los Angeles and New Orleans. *Not Enough Indians* is his first novel.